D0065900

The
MAGICIANS'
CHALLENGE

The
MAGICIANS'
CHALLENGE

Tom McGowen

◆ ◆ ◆

LODESTAR BOOKS ◆ Dutton ◆ New York

No character in this book is intended to represent any actual person; all the incidents of the story are entirely fictional in nature.

Library of Congress Cataloging-in-Publication Data

McGowen, Tom.
  The magicians' challenge/Tom McGowen.
    p. cm.
  "Lodestar books."
  Summary: The magician Armindor and his young apprentice Tigg travel south to their home city of Ingarron to continue humanity's battle against the intelligent ratlike creatures known as reen, who lurk in many of the world's cities and plan a bloody takeover. Sequel to "The Magician's Company."
  ISBN 0-525-67289-3
  [1. Fantasy.] I. Title.   89-32333
PZ7.M47849Mah 1989   CIP
[Fic]—dc20   AC

Published in the United States by Lodestar Books, an affiliate of Dutton Children's Books, a division of Penguin Books USA Inc.

Published simultaneously in Canada by Fitzhenry & Whiteside Limited, Toronto

Editor: Rosemary Brosnan

Printed in the U.S.A.   First Edition

10 9 8 7 6 5 4 3 2 1

for Jaclyn,
my grandniece and ardent fan

· · · 1 · · ·

With a steady *creak-shush, creak-shush* of rising and falling oars, the merchant ship *Smiling Squid* glided out of the harbor of the port city of Inbal and pushed its prow into the Silver Sea. At opposite sides of the stern, the captain and first mate leaned their weight on the long handles of the big steering paddles, and with skill gained from years of experience guided the ship onto an invisible path through the sun-speckled water that would take it straight to the distant port of Orrello, across the sea.

After a time the captain judged the *Smiling Squid* to be well on course and heaved his paddle into a neutral position, as did the mate. "Up oars," bawled the captain, and the rows of oarsmen along each side of the ship lifted their oars up from the water and slid them inboard. "Lower sail!" As a handful of seamen darted toward the single mast to carry out his second order, Captain P'gim gave a satisfied sigh, crammed a wad of aromatic chewing weed into his mouth, and turned his gaze toward his passengers.

It wasn't unusual for merchant ships to carry passengers—that was the only way for anyone to get across the Silver Sea. But such passengers were generally independent merchants traveling on business, or low-ranking noblemen acting as messengers between rulers of distant cities, and the passengers that had come aboard the *Smiling Squid* this morning certainly didn't seem to fit into either of those categories. Captain P'gim wasn't quite sure what to make of them.

They were standing together near the stern, watching the city of Inbal recede into the distance. There wasn't anything particularly remarkable about them. One was a dark-haired boy of about thirteen summers of age, another was a girl of about the same age, with orange-blonde hair, and the third was a tall, burly, elderly man wearing the ankle-length blue robe that marked him as a sage, a gatherer of magic and knowledge. There was also a grubber perched on the boy's shoulder—one of the furry, little, cat-sized creatures that had handlike paws and were said to be nearly as smart as people, although P'gim doubted that. It was undoubtedly a pet. No, there didn't seem to be anything really special about the little group, but it was quite clear to P'gim that they *were* special in some way. Their passage on his ship had been arranged by a servant of the High Chairman, ruler of Inbal, and the High Chairman himself, together with the High Master of the Inbal Guild of Sages, and several other important personages, had been on hand to see the passengers come on board and to bid them farewell. Who they were to receive such attention P'gim couldn't imagine, but being curious by nature he hoped to find out. Cocking his head slightly, he concentrated on overhearing their conversation.

"Well, say good-bye to your northland, Jilla," said the sage, whose name, P'gim knew, was Armindor. "You'll find the south very different." His voice was deep and pleasant. A narrow ring of snow-white hair encircled his otherwise bald head, but his face seemed oddly youthful despite his obvious age.

"You'll never see ice or snow again," the boy promised with a grin. His dark eyes were bright with intelligence, and he projected an air of self-confidence. "In Ingarron in the summertime, it gets so hot you can fry heron eggs in the sunlight on the paving stones of the main square!"

"You're fooling, Tigg," charged the girl, looking at him accusingly. She, too, seemed bright and alert to the watching P'gim. "He's fooling, isn't he, Armindor?"

"Not by much," said the sage, smiling. "A little light frost is usually the closest we get to ice or snow. He *is* exaggerating about frying eggs in sunlight, although it does get very hot sometimes."

P'gim nodded to himself. The twanging accents of the man and boy revealed that they came from far in the south, while the girl's speech showed she was a northerner, and from their words it was obvious they were all now going south together. Doubtless they were going to Orrello to join a trade caravan with which they could travel safely through the great expanse of wilderness between Orrello and the city of Ingarron, which seemed to be their final destination. But why had they made such a long journey from Ingarron to the northland in the first place, wondered the curious P'gim. Inbal was the northernmost port on the Silver Sea; north of it lay the backward Land of Wemms, now torn by a bloody civil war, and beyond Wemms was the vast wilderness known as the Wild Lands, a region teeming with dangerous animals and, it was said, horrible monsters, which was shunned by humans. What could there be in any of these places to bring a sage and his apprentice, which P'gim judged the dark-haired boy to be, all the way from Ingarron, a journey of several moons? And what made an old man and a pair of children so important that a great nobleman, the High Chairman of Inbal, would come to see them off?

"You can hardly see Inbal anymore," the girl, Jilla, was saying a trifle wistfully. She shaded her eyes with her hands. "We're getting farther and farther away."

Armindor put a hand inside his robe and brought forth an object which he handed to her. "Here. Look at it through the Spell of Far-seeing."

Captain P'gim's ears twitched. A spell? Ah, this sage must be a great magician!

The girl put the object to her eye. "It's marvelous!" she exclaimed after a moment. "I can never get over how it makes far things seem close. It's like we've jumped back toward Inbal!"

At that moment Armindor happened to glance around and caught sight of Captain P'gim staring toward the girl with undisguised curiosity and longing. "Would you like to experience a spell of ancient magic, Captain?" called the magician. "Come join us."

Delighted, P'gim hurried to them. Taking the magical object from Jilla, Armindor presented it to the seaman, who took it gingerly and examined it with great interest. It appeared to be a kind of long tube made of some unknown, smooth, red material.

"Put the small end to your eye," instructed Armindor, "and close the other eye. Look toward Inbal."

P'gim followed his instructions. "Great Badoween!" he exclaimed, invoking the name of the weather god worshipped by sailors. "It's like we were back in the harbor!"

He took the object from his eye and examined it again, gently stroking the smooth substance of which it was made. "I've never seen such craftsmanship! Did you make it, Your Wisdom?" he asked, using the polite form of address for sages.

"Ah, no one today can make such a thing," said Armindor wistfully. "This is an ancient spell, as I said, Captain. It was made in the Age of Magic."

P'gim's eyes widened. The Age of Magic was the time of legend, some three thousand years ago, when, it was said, every man, woman, and child in the world had been a magician. According to the old, old tales, there had been vast cities formed of shining towers that touched the clouds, and between the cities ran straight, smooth roads upon which people traveled at enormous speeds in magically powered vehicles. People had also been able to *fly*, to talk with one another across vast distances, to see things that were happening half the world away. And, it was said, there had been no hunger, sickness, or want in those times.

But something had happened. The tales described a terrible rain of fire from the sky, searing and shattering the cities and roads, and killing people by the countless thousands. Then had come what the legends called the Winter of Death, when the sky had turned dark both day and night, and the earth stayed frozen for several moons. Thousands more people had died, as well as countless numbers of animals of all kinds. No plants grew. Life had nearly vanished from the world.

But finally, the legends said, the darkness faded from the sky, and sunlight returned to warm the earth and thaw it. Seeds that had lain dormant in the ground now sprouted, and patches of green appeared and spread. Hibernating animals had awakened, and the few surviving humans had come creeping out of their shelters. However, with all the magic and knowledge now lost or destroyed, people had lived like savages for more than two thousand years. Only during the last five or six centuries had they begun to regain civilization. From time to time sages had puzzled out bits of ancient knowledge by studying old, old writings that had been copied and recopied from generation to generation, or had discovered ancient spells of magic that had been miraculously preserved through the scores of centuries. And now P'gim found himself holding such a discovery in his own hands.

"Badoween!" he exclaimed. "Where did you find such a marvel, Your Wisdom?"

"We found it in the Wild Lands," spoke up the boy, Tigg. P'gim stared at him, wondering if he were jesting.

"He speaks truly," said Armindor. "I learned of an ancient underground ruin in the Wild Lands, where a number of spells had been preserved since the time of the Fire from the Sky. My apprentice, Tigg, and I went there. We found this and a few other things."

Well, that explains why they came north, thought P'gim. He glanced from the man to the boy. They had great courage to brave the Wild Lands!

"You found other things, you say?" he queried. "Were they as wonderful as this?" He returned the Spell of Far-seeing to Armindor.

The magician grimaced. "We can be sure that they are, but unfortunately we have not been able to solve the use of all of them. You see, the ancients of the Age of Magic had so much more knowledge than we do, that many of their spells were for doing things that we can no longer even imagine. Like this, for instance." He reached into his robe and brought forth another object.

It was a small, round box, made out of the same smooth, unfamiliar material as the far-seeing tube. Captain P'gim thought it had no top, but when he gently tried to poke a finger into it, he found that it was covered over with a hard, nearly invisible substance. At the bottom of the box were some unknown symbols or designs arranged in a circle, and set in the exact center of the circle was a gleaming bluish thing somewhat resembling a slim knife blade with a sharp point. Although Armindor was holding the box perfectly still, the gleaming thing was spinning and shivering and jouncing in a way that made P'gim think of a restless insect. "Is it alive?" he whispered, peering at it in fascination.

"No," said the magician. "It will stop moving in a moment or two."

As P'gim watched, the thing finally did come to a stop. "Now," said Armindor, "think of it as a pointing finger. See where it is pointing?"

P'gim lifted his eyes, following the direction toward which the sharp-pointed end was aiming. "Straight toward Inbal," he observed.

"Watch," said Armindor. He turned so that he was facing in the opposite direction. As he moved, the pointed thing in the box again jittered and spun, gradually subsiding when he stopped moving. "Look," said Armindor. "It is still pointing toward Inbal." P'gim saw that this was true.

Armindor moved a few steps to one side, beckoning the seaman to follow. Again when the pointer came to a stop it was pointing straight toward the receding port city. "You see?" said Armindor. "No matter where I stand, no matter where I might place this, no matter if the ship were five thousand paces to either side from where it is, this point would still be aimed straight in the direction where Inbal lies. If we were standing *in* Inbal, it would be pointing in the same direction, toward the northland beyond." He shrugged. "Why it always points in that direction we don't know, and what this spell could have been used for, we cannot imagine."

P'gim rubbed his bearded chin thoughtfully. "Well, I can think of a way *I* could use it. If I were out in the middle of the Silver Sea in a bad fog and couldn't see the stars or any of the other things sailors use to find their way, I could stay on course to Inbal just by keeping the ship headed in the direction this thing points!" He paused and shrugged. "Of course, it wouldn't be of any use if I wanted to get to some place *other* than Inbal."

Armindor stared at him. "That's an interesting idea, though. The possibility that this could be a spell for finding the way from one place to another had never occurred to me before. You've given me something to think about."

"Well, I'm glad to have been of help, Your Wisdom," said P'gim, congratulating himself on having gained the magician's goodwill. Now perhaps he could get answers to all the other things he was curious about. "So, now you're going home with all your finds, eh?"

"Yes, home to Ingarron," the magician acknowledged. "But first we have to take care of some important business in Orrello. I must visit the ruler of Orrello and talk with him."

P'gim shifted his lump of chewing weed from one cheek to the other and eyed the sage speculatively. "Um . . . well . . . that may not be easy, Your Wisdom. The Lord Director of Orrello won't talk to just *anybody*, if you'll pardon my saying so."

"He'll talk to us," Armindor assured the seaman. "We have a letter for him from the High Chairman of Inbal, urging him to listen carefully to what we have to say. We have some important information concerning the safety of his city!"

"Oh?" Captain P'gim spat a mouthful of weed juice up into the wind, where it was carried far out over the side of the ship. "Is Orrello in some kind of danger?"

"Orrello and every other human community is in danger," Armindor told him grimly. "Have you heard of the creatures called reen, and of what happened in Inbal?"

"A bit," said P'gim. "I was told there were creatures found living in the sewers of the city, and they caused some kind of trouble. They're some sort of smart rat, I understand."

"They're much more than that," said Armindor. "They aren't merely animals, their ancestors were some of those that were changed by the Fire from the Sky, as the old tales claim, and the reen are now as smart as we are! They have been secretly living among us for centuries, and they know our ways and can speak our language. Tigg and I learned of them in the Wild Lands, where some of them had followed us to try to get the spells we found. They tried to steal the spells from us in Inbal, and they even attacked the Inbal Sages' Guildhall, where the spells were in safekeeping. The High Chairman's Peacekeeper guardsmen fought a battle with them and finally drove them off, but I fear that battle was the start of a war! The reen intend to wipe us humans out, Captain; they're going to rise up in all our cities someday and do their best to massacre us!"

P'gim stood with his mouth open, forgetting to chew. Recollecting himself after a moment, he spat again and regarded Armindor with concern. "But they couldn't do that, could they, Your Wisdom?"

"Perhaps they could if they caught us by surprise," said Armindor. "That is why I must alert the rulers of Orrello and Ingarron and every other city to the danger. The High Chairman of Inbal learned about the reen in time to begin taking steps against them, but the rulers of other cities don't know anything about the creatures. They must be warned before it is too late!"

··· 2 ···

P'gim opened his mouth to ask a question, but at that moment the first mate called to him from the front of the vessel, and the captain hurried off to his duties. Armindor watched him go, then glanced down at the round red box that he still held in his hands.

"Did you hear what he said about this, Tigg?" the magician asked. "Do you suppose it *could* somehow be a spell for finding your way from one place to another?"

"But it's as he said—the spell wouldn't be any good unless you wanted to go straight to where the pointer points," protested the apprentice. "What's the good of only being able to find your way straight north?" Then he paused, and his eyes widened. "Wait—that's it!" he suddenly shouted.

"What?" asked the startled Armindor and Jilla at the same time.

"Look, we know that the pointed end of the thing always points north," Tigg explained, his eyes blazing with excitement. "Well, that means the other end is always pointing straight south. So then, the direction straight to the right of the pointer has to be east, and the direction straight to the left has to be west! You see how the spell could work? No matter where you were in the world, whether in the middle of a sea, or the middle of a forest, and no matter whether you could see the sun or moon or stars or any other way of locating direction, you could always tell exactly where each direction is by looking at the pointer!"

"I think you've got it," Armindor said after a moment, his voice rising in exultation. He was so excited that his hands were shaking, making the pointer quiver. "It makes sense. I always wondered why four of these symbols in the circle around the pointer were bigger than the others, but I can see now that they must stand for the four main directions. Look, if I turn the box so that the pointer is pointing straight at the symbol that looks like a wriggling snake, then the other three line up exactly where they should be if they were the other directions. These symbols must stand for the ancient names for north, south, east, and west!"

"But what are the smaller ones in between each of the bigger ones?" wondered Jilla.

"That fits, too—they can only be the symbols for the directions in between the main ones," Armindor explained. "The directions sailors call northeast, northwest, southeast, and southwest. There's no doubt; this *is* a spell for finding your way! You could find your way exactly toward any direction just by walking, or steering a ship, toward any of the symbols, as long as the pointer is pointing at the symbol for north."

"But we don't really know which symbol stands for north," Tigg protested. "It might not have been that snaky one for the ancients. Maybe it's really one of the others."

"We can never know for sure," Armindor agreed, "but it doesn't actually matter. For us, the symbol of the snake will stand for north." He put a hand on the boy's shoulder. "Tigg, you've done it again, as you did with the Spell of Far-seeing. You've figured out how an ancient spell works. I think you're going to be one of the greatest magicians in the history of the Guild of Sages!" The boy squirmed in embarrassed pride, while Jilla beamed at him.

It was a five-day voyage across the Silver Sea from Inbal to Orrello. Although called a sea, the Silver Sea was actually a gigantic lake, which had been formed out of the Great Lakes as a result of the titanic thermonuclear catastrophe that had shattered and altered the North American continent three thousand years earlier. Thus, its waters were generally calmer and more even than those of the high seas, and none of the three human travelers or their grubber companion suffered from seasickness. Armindor, Tigg, and Reepah the grubber had made the trip before, of course, on their way to the far northern Wild Lands, and so it was not a new experience for them. But for Jilla, who had never dreamed of leaving the northland until, less than half a year ago, she had been adopted by Armindor following the death of her family, the first day on the sea was full of newness and excitement. She was awed by the vast expanse of blue gray water that seemed to extend forever in all directions, and was thrilled by the glimpses she caught of sea life, such as the small, multicolored hexopuses, which often floated in clusters at the surface of the water with their six long, stringlike tentacles spread out around them. With the Spell of Far-seeing she studied the flocks of broad-winged, seagoing daybats that soared along behind the ship to feed upon refuse that was thrown overboard, and once she caught sight of a sea turtle, half as big as the ship, swimming swiftly past in the distance. But by the next day, much of the excitement had worn off, and Jilla was content to sit cross-legged on the deck, talking with Tigg, Armindor, and, to the amazement of the crew, Reepah.

On the morning of the fourth day, the travelers emerged from the small tent that had been put up on deck for their shelter and privacy, and saw that P'gim, the first mate, and most of the crewmen were clustered at the front of the ship, staring out across the sea. Curious, the man and the two youngsters, with Reepah perched on Tigg's shoulder, made their way forward to see what was happening.

"Something wrong, Captain?" asked Armindor.

P'gim, jaw bulging with the ever-present wad of chewing weed, glanced at the sage and jerked his head in the direction toward which all the sailors were peering. "See out there straight ahead on the horizon—that brownish smudge? We can't figure out what it is. Never seen anything like it before."

"I see it," said Tigg. "It must be something floating in the water."

"Could it be some kind of monster?" asked Jilla, almost hopefully. There were many tales of monsters in the Silver Sea.

P'gim gave a dry chuckle. "I've sailed these waters for twenty summers, Little Maid, and I've never seen a monster yet. As for something floating in the water, boy, it would have to be mighty, mighty *big!* It's *far,* and for us to see it at such a distance it must be many hundreds of paces wide and nearly as high." He spat out into the water. "But whatever it is, it's in the exact spot we're heading for, right in the direction of Orrello."

"Perhaps I can solve the mystery," said Armindor. "I can't make out what it is with my own eyes, but the Spell of Far-seeing may reach that distance." He took the red tube from inside his robe, adjusted it, and put it to his eye. For a long time he peered through the spell while the others watched him with curiosity. At last he said, "I believe it is smoke. A great cloud of smoke."

"Smoke?" P'gim chewed thoughtfully at his wad of weed. "Then it could either be a burning ship or a big fire in Orrello!" He turned to a seaman standing beside him. "Gyl, get up into the birdnest and keep an eye on that smoke until you can make out what's causing it." Tigg and Jilla watched with interest as the sailor swarmed up a rope ladder to the enclosed platform, like an upside-down bell, high near the top of the mast. From there he would be better able to tell what was causing the mysterious smoke cloud as the ship drew nearer to it.

The *Smiling Squid* crew dispersed and went about its business, while the boy, girl, man, and grubber squatted on the deck and had their breakfast of bread and smoked fish, provided by the ship's cook and storekeeper, who was P'gim's wife. Their breakfast conversation focused on the smoke cloud.

"There is a great deal of forest around Orrello," commented Armindor. "Perhaps there is a forest fire. I hope it is not a fire in the city!"

"I do not like it," said Reepah, the grubber, in his squeaky voice. "I have a bad feeling about it!" The others looked at him with sudden concern, for they had learned that the grubber was often able to sense impending trouble. He was not at all a pet, as P'gim had thought him to be, but a brave and intelligent companion of the humans. Tigg had found him the previous summer, lying badly injured from an attack by an animal, and the boy and Armindor had nursed him back to health and full strength. He had been tremendously helpful on their journey to the Wild Lands, and had chosen to stay with them and help them with their quest to alert humans to the danger of the reen, who were also age-old enemies of the grubber race.

During most of the afternoon, Armindor, the two youngsters, and Reepah stayed at the front of the ship, peering anxiously at the brown pall of smoke that could now clearly be seen for what it was.

"That's a lot of smoke," Tigg commented. "It must be a big fire. If it's in Orrello, the whole city must be burning!"

"Hoi, the deck," yelled the man up in the birdnest suddenly. "There are ships coming toward us. I can make out at least six."

"Why would so many ships be sailing together?" wondered Tigg.

"It sounds as if it might be a war fleet," said Armindor in a worried voice. "By the beard of Roodemiss, could Orrello be at war? Has it been attacked and burned by someone's war fleet?"

P'gim and most of the *Smiling Squid* crew crowded at the front of the ship, staring at the distant ships, visible as specks against the background of smoke. "They're not sailing close together like a war fleet would," observed the first mate, Durvn. "They're scattered."

"Yes," muttered P'gim. "What in Badoween's name is going on?"

Minutes passed. Then there was a call from the birdnest. "Hoi, on the deck. They're merchant ships. I can recognize the *Wind Witch* and the *Wave Dancer.*"

"Come on, Durvn, let's get on the steering paddles," said P'gim. "We'll get within hailing distance of one of them and see if we can find out about all this."

Skillfully handling the big paddles at the bow, the two men altered the *Smiling Squid*'s course until it was headed toward the closest ship, now clearly visible, which was sailing toward them. P'gim hauled his paddle to neutral position and leaned out over the side of the ship, watching the approaching vessel. When it was about a hundred paces away, he cupped his hand to his mouth and yelled out, "Hoi, *Wave Dancer*—what's burning back there? Where are you all going?"

After a moment, everyone on the *Smiling Squid* heard, faint but clear, the reply.

"Turn back, *Smiling Squid!* Orrello's burning! It's been taken over by a horde of some kind of rat-things. They killed almost everybody. We managed to get away and we're going to Inbal."

"Rat-things!" exclaimed Tigg. "He must mean—"

"The reen," said Armindor through clenched teeth. "Their uprising has begun."

P'gim turned to look at the magician, eyes wide. "Badoween's breath!" he cursed. "You were right, Your Wisdom. Those reen things you told me of are making war on us!" He strode a few paces in toward the center of the deck, stopped, and savagely rubbed his thatch of hair as he glared about, trying to collect his thoughts. "Well, we dare not go to Orrello now. We must turn back, as *Wave Dancer*'s captain advises. There'll be no profit for this voyage!" He raised his voice and began to shout orders. "Rowers to your oars. Up sail."

"Wait," called Armindor. "Captain, we must get to Ingarron. You must drop us off on the coast somewhere south of Orrello."

P'gim stared at him. "Begging your pardon, Your Wisdom, but you're out of your mind. There's only one road to Ingarron from the coast, and it leads out of Orrello and runs far inland. You could never find your way to it from some other part of the coast. There's probably tens of thousands of paces of wilderness between the coast and the road, and you'd just get lost and wander about until you died!"

Armindor shook his head. "We have found that the spell I showed you a few days ago is a Spell of Wayfinding, and we can use it to make our way to the road. We'll need provisions, though, so we'll buy all you can spare. But we *must* get to Ingarron, Captain P'gim, so that we can prevent what has happened in Orrello from happening there—if it's not too late already! The people of Ingarron must be warned against the danger of the reen!"

Captain P'gim hesitated a moment longer, then shrugged. "Well, if you're willing to risk it and think you can make it, it's your own fate in your hands. I can let you have provisions for about six days." He raised his voice to give more orders. "Oarsmen, start your stroke. First Mate Durvn to the starside steering paddle. We'll drop these people twenty thousand paces down the coast from Orrello. That should be enough. And may Badoween and all their own gods look after them!"

· · · 3 · · ·

At mid morning the next day, the three humans and
their grubber companion stood on a pebbled beach
and watched the *Smiling Squid* grow smaller as it
headed back out across the Silver Sea. Around their
feet were piled a number of bulging sacks, and Armindor, Tigg, and Jilla each had a full water bag,
supplied by Captain P'gim, slung from their shoulders.

"All right, let's get started," Armindor urged, turning away from the view of the ship. "First, we'd best
go through our belongings and get rid of anything
we can. It will be hard going until we get to the road,
and the more we have to carry the harder it will be."

When they finished, there was a pile of discarded
clothing and a few other things lying on the beach,
and each of the humans held a single sack containing
a portion of the food supply and valuables and neces-
sities, such as Armindor's spell-books, the ancient
magical objects he and Tigg had found in the Wild
Lands, the letter from the High Chairman of Inbal,

cooking utensils, and so on. Jilla's sack also contained her puppets, her last link to the aunts and uncle who had reared her and who had been traveling puppeteers. In addition to his sack, Tigg carried a loaded crossbow that had once served him well in the Wild Lands.

Armindor balanced the Spell of Way-finding in his hand, allowing the pointer to come to a stop. He carefully turned the box until the pointer was aimed straight at the symbol he and Tigg had decided would stand for north. "Orrello is straight up the coastline to the north," he muttered, "and the road from it to Ingarron angles south. So to reach it, we must head straight west—toward this symbol that looks like a line with three shorter lines sticking out of one side of it." He faced in that direction, slipped the spell back into the deep pocket inside his robe, and shifted his sack into a comfortable position over his shoulder. "Let us be off, then, and may Roodemiss be with us."

The beach was no more than a few hundred paces wide, and beyond it rose the great shaggy-green wall of a vast forest. The day was sunny and bright, but upon entering the forest the travelers found themselves immersed in green gloom. The trees grew close together, and their intertwining branches overhead shut out most of the sunlight.

"Do you suppose there are lots of animals in these woods?" Jilla asked. Never having been in a forest before, she was rather uneasy.

"A great many, I'm sure," said Armindor, "but

most of them are small and harmless, I assure you." This wasn't quite true, but the magician did not wish to worry the girl. Actually, as he knew, there were likely to be a number of large, dangerous creatures in a wilderness such as this.

"I will ko ahead of you and make sure all is well," said Reepah, trotting off. Soon he was out of their sight. The humans were glad to have him act as a scout, for they knew he possessed a marvelous sense of smell that could help guard them against danger, and being a creature that had been born into the wilderness and spent his life in it, he was wise in its ways.

Armindor's assurances, plus the fact that she neither saw nor heard anything other than flying insects and an occasional bird call, made Jilla less fearful. On the other hand, Tigg, who had traveled through the vast and dangerous forest of the Wild Lands, was nervously alert, and he saw a number of things that went unnoticed by the girl. A pointed-eared, brown-and-black-striped creature about the size of Reepah stared down at the humans as they passed beneath the branch upon which it crouched. A sharp black nose, beneath a pair of beady black eyes, poked out of a nearby clump of underbrush and twitched, sniffing at the travelers' scent. And once, the boy caught sight of a pair of faintly glowing yellow eyes staring at him from a thickly shadowed place some thirty paces back among the trees. Tigg estimated that the eyes were nearly as high off the ground as his own, indicating that the creature was quite large, and the boy lifted the crossbow, putting his finger on the trigger, in case the animal should attack. But the eyes stayed where they were, staring for a few moments more, then blinked and vanished.

The three travelers tramped steadily along in single file, not pausing for a midday meal. From time to time Armindor would halt to consult the Spell of Wayfinding to make sure they were still moving in the right direction, then they would march on.

When the forest began to darken around them, the magician stopped and swung the sack from his shoulder to the ground. "It will soon be night," he observed. "Let's make a campfire while we can still see what we're doing, and then we'll have a bite of supper."

He had chosen a tiny, almost circular clearing in the middle of a cluster of trees that had the comforting effect of a circular wall. Shortly, a fire was crackling. Reepah materialized out of the darkness, and soon the humans were enjoying a supper of dried, salted meat and toasted bread chunks dipped into vegetable paste, while Reepah munched on plain toasted bread.

All these provisions, bought from P'gim, were of course from northern Inbal. "This northern vegetable paste isn't spicy enough," grumbled Tigg. "I'll be glad when we're back in Ingarron, where people know how to make it right!"

"How long will it take us to get to Ingarron?" asked Jilla.

"I estimate that we should reach the road in another two or three days," Armindor told her. "After that, I fear we shall have a good fifteen to twenty days of steady walking."

"Fifteen to twenty days?" Jilla stopped chewing and stared at him in dismay. "We'll run out of food!"

"There is plenty food all around," Reepah assured her. "I will find it."

"He can," acknowledged Tigg. "He kept us both well fed for days when he and I were in the Wild Lands when we got separated from Armindor that time I told you about. He found mushrooms, bird eggs, all kinds of tasty roots—lots of things."

Tired out from their day of walking, they fell right to sleep. They kept no watch, for Armindor and Tigg knew that Reepah's sense of smell would awaken him if anything dangerous came near them.

The next morning they ate a simple meal of bread and water, and packed up their belongings. Armindor checked the Spell of Way-finding, to get them headed in the right direction, and once again they were off.

Near noon they encountered a setback. Reepah, who had been scouting ahead, returned with bad news. "There is water ahead. Much."

They trudged over ground that became noticeably more muddy, until finally water was actually oozing up over their feet at each step. The trees were farther apart in this area, and peering ahead the travelers saw that there was an expanse of water that extended for an unknown distance forward and to both sides. Huge trees with parts of their thick, twisting roots exposed rose here and there out of the motionless surface of the water. The air was lively with the shrill whine of insects, the croaking of frogs, and other sounds.

"A swamp," said Armindor. "Roodemiss curse it, this is a piece of bad luck. We'll have to try to find our way around it. I hope it isn't very wide."

"Couldn't we just wade through it?" questioned Tigg. "It can't be very deep—there are trees growing in it."

Armindor shook his head. "It's deeper than it looks, and a swamp is generally filled with dangerous things—poisonous snakes and insects and other creatures. No, we must go around it. We will turn south, because at least that will have us heading in the direction of Ingarron, and simply keep going until we can head west again."

Turning, they began to plod southward through the mud. The edge of the swamp teemed with life. Huge dragonflies, their bodies glinting metallically red, blue, and green, darted and hovered in the air, each patrolling above its own small section of water. Ahead of the travelers a pair of walking fish trotted through the mud on their four splayed, misshapen legs, and slid into the swamp. Jilla saw, farther out in the water, a froglike head nearly as big as her own, staring at her with golden goggle eyes. A green-and-black-striped snake, as thick as her thumb and as long as her arm, glided with lightning speed past her foot and vanished from sight in the underbrush.

Somewhere far out in the swamp, something bellowed. It was a fearsome sound, deep and vibrating, that suggested an enormous animal. "Roodemiss's teeth, I wonder what that was?" muttered Armindor.

They came to a cluster of plants: long, green stems topped with swirls of spiky leaves rose up out of the water at the very edge of the swamp. Reepah, who had been scouting ahead, was waiting here for his companions. He yanked up one of the plants and peeled away the outer sheath of stem at the bottom, revealing a bulbous white root. "Kood to eat," he assured the humans, and bit into the root with a loud crunch. Armindor, Tigg, and Jilla each pulled up a plant, peeled it as the grubber had shown them, and with various degrees of timidity, sampled the root. They found it to have a crisp, tangy taste that was most pleasant. For a time they all stood, plucking, peeling, and munching until they were sated. Then they continued on.

Early in the afternoon Armindor stopped to check the Spell of Way-finding. "We appear to be moving in a southwesterly direction," he announced. "That could mean we've reached the southern end of the swamp and will be able to head straight west again soon."

Reepah suddenly appeared. "There is strange smell

ahead," he said. "Little like smell of snake but much more strong. I think we must be careful."

Clustering together they went on, moving more slowly and cautiously. After a time Jilla said, "Look— is that a *village?*" Far in the distance a number of dome-shaped objects were visible at the edge of the swamp. They were obviously not natural features of the landscape.

"They certainly look like something made by people," said Armindor. "Huts of some kind."

"No," declared the grubber. "Not people things. The strange smell comes from there. Not a hyoo-men smell."

They advanced to within only a few hundred paces of the dome-shaped structures and halted, looking the things over. The nearest structure was about twice as high as Armindor, and appeared to be made out of plant leaves, stems, and roots packed together and held in place with dried mud. Some fifty paces beyond it was another dome, and the travelers could see still others farther on. The humans were now aware of the odor Reepah had spoken of; a musky, faintly unpleasant smell.

Suddenly, a gigantic form burst out of the water and bounded onto the land between the four travelers and the nearest dome. The three humans screamed in terror, and the grubber gave a frightened yelp. Facing them was a hideous monster. More than twenty paces long and half a dozen high, it stood on four legs as thick as young tree trunks. Its huge head consisted mainly of a pair of long, tapering jaws that bristled with jagged, sharp-pointed teeth. Its greenish-brown body was covered with a pattern of bumpy scales, and a row of thick, bony spikes sprouted along its back and down the long, tapering tail that dragged on the ground behind it. It glared at the travelers with baleful yellow eyes, and opened its jaws to emit an earsplitting bellow like the one they had heard earlier. The same atomic radiation that had changed the rat ancestors of the reen and Reepah's prairie dog ancestors had caused this thing's alligator ancestors to give rise to a creature that could have rivaled a dinosaur.

"Quick, make for the trees!" yelled Tigg. "It can't get at us there."

The humans and Reepah fled to the forest that edged the swamp, heading back to the closer-growing trees where the monster couldn't squeeze through after them. It launched itself in a lumbering charge and followed them a short distance, stopping only when it could no longer move easily between tree trunks. Then it stood and glared toward the cluster of trees where the travelers had taken refuge.

"That's as bad as any creature I ever saw in the Wild Lands," Tigg commented. "If it had caught us out in the open, without any trees to hide in, we'd be dead now!"

"I wish it would go away," said Jilla, a slight quaver in her voice.

Almost as if in answer to her wish, something

happened at that moment to divert the creature's attention. From the nearest of the mounds at the swamp edge came a faint bleating sound. Instantly, the giant reptile's head swung around, and it regarded the mound intently. After a few moments the bleating sound came again.

In two loping steps the reptile reached the mound, and with its teeth began tearing away chunks from the top of the structure. Through the opening it made, a small creature came squirming out of the inside of the mound. Not much bigger than Reepah, it was a stubby, miniature version of the giant reptile. It opened its mouth and bleated.

The giant reptile continued to tear open the mound. Another small reptile appeared from within it.

"Why, it's a nest," marveled Armindor, watching the scene with interest. "The creatures must lay eggs and build the domes around them. The big one must be the mother of the ones in that nest."

"We should *ko,* now!" urged Reepah, sounding somewhat exasperated and tugging at the magician's robe.

"Yes, of course. Let's get away from here while the thing is occupied," said Armindor. "We'd better stay back among these close-growing trees; we don't want to get near any of the other mounds. There are probably mothers lurking in the water near each one."

Moving as quickly as they could, they fled from the

sight and sound of the mother reptile freeing her babies from the nest. From time to time they would edge a little closer to the swamp to see if they were yet clear of the nesting area, but there were a good many of the mounds ranged along the edge of the water, and it was late in the day before the four companions had passed them all and left them far behind. Finally, Armindor halted.

"I think we're safe, now," he said. "I want to check the spell and see where we are."

He took the round box from the pocket of his robe, held it steady until the pointer came to a stop, and carefully aligned the pointer to the symbol for north. Tigg and Jilla, watching him, saw his face light up.

"Thanks be to Roodemiss!" he exclaimed. "Things aren't too bad after all. We must have come around the end of the swamp, for we're headed the exact way we want to go. We probably haven't lost more than half a day—maybe not even that much, for we've been heading southward, so we must be closer to Ingarron."

He regarded the girl and boy thoughtfully as he tucked the spell back into his pocket. He had been through many adventures with Tigg and knew that his young apprentice was brave, tough, and resourceful. Jilla, too, had shown, during the events that had taken place while they were staying in Inbal, that she was courageous and spirited. But he could see that they were both still shaken from the frightful experience with the giant reptile, and he felt sure they must be tired and hungry. I'm certainly tired, he thought. I'm really much too old to have to be running for my life from an angry monster!

He glanced about. "It's getting dark, isn't it? Perhaps we could camp here for the night. Are we far enough away from those swamp creatures to be safe, Reepah? Can you still smell them?"

"Far away," the grubber replied. "We are safe here."

Stooping, Armindor began to rummage through the sack he had been carrying. "It's a good thing none of us dropped our bags when we were running from that creature, eh? We still have a goodly amount of provisions. It's been a hard day and we're lucky to be alive; let's have a good supper, a good sleep, and if luck stays with us, perhaps in another day or two we shall reach the road."

· · · 4 · · ·

Early the next day the travelers were able to fill their waterbags from a little stream that they waded across in the forest. They were still in the forest at nightfall, and their supper consisted of toasted bread and raw mushrooms that Reepah had gathered from the forest floor.

By afternoon of the following day they became aware that they were gradually moving uphill and that the trees were thinning out around them. By late afternoon they were out of the forest and moving across open meadowland, where they camped for the night. At mid morning of the next day they reached the road.

It was not really much of a road—actually nothing more than a narrow dirt track that had been worn through the meadowland over many centuries by the passage of merchant caravans, bands of plodding migrants, and an occasional army. But it led straight south to the city of Ingarron, and there was no longer any need for Armindor to consult the Spell of Way-finding. All the travelers had to do now was to follow the road and it would take them home.

Nor was there any longer a need for Reepah to scout ahead, for the trail ran through open, level ground, and there was a clear view in all directions. But the grubber's nose still proved more useful than anyone's eyes. From his perch on Tigg's shoulder he leaned forward and sniffed. "Far ahead is hyoo-man and one of the horned, four-foot runners that hyoo-mens ride," he announced.

Armindor frowned slightly. "A rider on a horn-beast? It is strange that a rider is on the road alone. Well, if it is someone heading for Orrello, we can save them the rest of their trip."

A short time later they could make out the horn-beast. It did not appear to be coming up the trail toward them, but instead seemed to be well off to one side, moving a step or two from time to time as it browsed. There was no one on its back.

"I can't see a person anywhere," said Jilla, shading her eyes with her hands.

Nor could they see anyone as they drew nearer. It was only when they were almost abreast of the horn-beast that Reepah pointed with a handlike paw. "There—lying in the krass!"

Looking where he pointed, the others saw that someone was lying facedown a few paces off on one side of the trail. The tall grass that covered most of the meadow nearly hid the inert form.

Tigg and Jilla darted to the figure. "It's a man," Jilla called to Armindor. "A young man."

"Is he dead?" Armindor hurried to join them.

But at that moment the man lifted his head and rolled his eyes toward the figures clustered over him. "Wah-ter," he pleaded, in a voice that was little more than a wheezing whisper.

Tigg quickly unslung the waterbag from his shoulder, pulled out the wooden plug that stoppered it, and tilted it to the man's mouth. The man struggled to pull himself up on one elbow. He made harsh gulping sounds as he swallowed, and the travelers realized that he must have been nearly dying of thirst.

After a time he ceased to gulp, and gave a long, shuddering sigh. "My thanks to you, friends," he said in a weak voice. "And my thanks to almighty Garmood for sending you this way."

Armindor studied him. He was a young man in his twenties, and from the look of his clothing he was moderately wealthy. His knee-length smock was of fine orange-dyed material, and the wrappings that covered his legs from knee to ankle were strips of an amber-colored fur. He had a pleasant, attractive face, with the same dark eyes, dark hair, and tan skin as Tigg and Armindor, which indicated that he, too, was probably a citizen of Ingarron.

"Who are you?" asked the magician. "How do you happen to be on the road alone?" This was most unusual, for the countryside between cities teemed with dangers, and travelers always journeyed in large groups.

The young man laboriously raised himself to a sitting position. "My name is tiLammis, Your Wisdom. As to what I am doing here, why, I was trying to get home to Ingarron. I have been living in Orrello, and I was fleeing from there! You probably won't believe me, but I tell you that Orrello has been attacked by a horde of creatures that looked like big rats, except that they walked on two legs and carried weapons. They were killing everyone on sight!"

Armindor settled himself into a cross-legged position on the ground, facing tiLammis. "We believe you. We know of these creatures. They are called reen. How did the attack take place?"

"It was just about sunset. Suddenly, the streets were full of the things! I don't know where they came from. They carried long tubes that they would lift up to their faces and point at people. Then the person they were pointing at would fall down dead. Those must have been magical weapons."

"Not at all," said Armindor. "The reen blow little darts out of the tubes, with puffs of breath, and the darts are poisoned."

"How did you manage to escape?" asked Tigg.

TiLammis turned his gaze to the boy. "I was on my hornbeast and I was just riding through the city gate when the creatures appeared. I was coming from a meeting with someone outside the city, and she had ridden ahead of me." His face took on a stricken look.

"I fear she must be dead now!" He fought, visibly, to hold back tears. "Anyway, when I saw what was happening, I quickly turned my hornbeast back through the gate and rode a ways outside the city, to save myself. A few other people managed to get out, too, and I rode among them hoping to find Allinis, my friend, but . . . We all waited for a time, hoping that the city Peacekeepers would overcome the creatures and restore order. Then we saw that the city was afire, and there seemed to be no hope left. Most of the others headed for the forest, but I decided I ought to return home to Ingarron. I had no provisions but a bottle of berry wine left over from the picnic Allinis and I had shared, but I finished it by the end of the second day on the road, so I've had nothing to drink the last few days except dew I sucked off the grass each morning, and I've had nothing to eat since the night I left Orrello."

"You need food, then," said Armindor. He rummaged in his sack and pulled out the last of the bread from Inbal, half a loaf, which he handed to tiLammis. The young man wolfed it down almost without chewing, despite its hardness.

"My thanks again," he said earnestly when he finished. "I would have died if you hadn't come along." He looked from Armindor to Tigg. "You two are Ingarronians also, aren't you? What are *you* doing out here by yourselves? And how did you know about the things that attacked Orrello?"

"That is a long story that we will tell you later,"

Armindor replied. "For now, let me merely introduce us. I am Armindor the Magician, High Master of the Sages' Guild of Ingarron. This is my apprentice, Tigg. This is Jilla, and that is Reepah, whom you will find to be as intelligent as any human. We, too, are on our way to Ingarron, and will be happy to have you travel with us."

"I am grateful for your help and delighted to join you," declared tiLammis. He began to struggle to get to his feet, and Tigg and Jilla hurried to help him. "Thanks," he told them. "I'm weak from hunger and thirst."

"Tigg, go and get the hornbeast," said Armindor. "Our friend had better ride until he gets his strength back." As Tigg sped off, Armindor looked thoughtfully at tiLammis. "You are an Ingarronian, but you say you were living in Orrello. Were you perhaps a merchant's representative there?"

"Exactly," the young man nodded. "I am—I was—the representative in Orrello of the Pynjo Merchandising Company of Ingarron. Master Merchant Pynjo is my uncle."

"Ah," murmured Armindor. Pynjo was one of the wealthiest and most influential merchants of Ingarron. It was a stroke of luck that his nephew was an eyewitness to the reen massacre of Orrello; this would lend tremendous weight to Armindor's attempts to alert the leaders of Ingarron to the danger from the reen.

"We shall travel on for a while, then stop around

midday for a bit to eat," said Armindor, as Tigg returned with the hornbeast. "I'm sure you are still very hungry and would like to eat more right now, tiLammis, but you mustn't eat too much all at once or you'll become sick." Tigg and Jilla helped the young merchant onto his mount, and once again the travelers were on their way, now five in number and with a hornbeast.

So began the long journey to Ingarron. Day after day they walked steadily along, through sunshine and rain, while the vast coastal forest receded behind them and finally was lost from sight. The last of the provisions they had purchased from Captain P'gim were gone by the second day on the road, but true to his promise, Reepah kept them well supplied with wild plant foods from the countryside through which they passed, and each evening they set snares for small birds or animals, which occasionally gained them enough meat for a stew or soup, cooked in the single clay pot that Armindor carried in his sack. They rationed their water carefully, but on their fifth day on the road they came to the spring known as the Traveler's Well, which was a regular watering place for merchant caravans, and there they filled up the waterbags again. On rainy nights they left the cooking pot in the open to fill with rainwater. No one got any fatter during the journey, but no one starved or went thirsty, and tiLammis gained back enough strength to be able to walk and lead the hornbeast, upon which

Armindor, Tigg, and Jilla piled their sacks of belongings.

The journey was uneventful and at times actually boring, as the countryside continued to be unvarying meadowland with little of interest in it to look at. There were many tales of travelers on the road between Ingarron and Orrello being attacked by dangerous wild beasts, and when caravans stopped for the night they formed protective circles and were guarded by watchful sentries, but the magician and his companions neither saw nor heard anything unusual, and Reepah's nose never once warned of danger.

However, on the sixteenth day of the journey, Reepah began to grow noticeably excited. "We are entering the land of my community," he announced. "I can smell my people."

"I thought this place seemed familiar," said Tigg, glancing about. It had been near this part of the trail, more than a year ago at the start of his and Armindor's long journey, that he had found Reepah lying injured in the meadow. Memories flooded into the boy's mind.

Memories were flooding into Reepah's mind, as well. "I must ko to my community," he squeaked. "I want to see old Tikatee akain, and Eenap and Teekah!"

"Of course you do—we understand, Reepah," Tigg told him. "Go ahead and visit your home. We'll keep going and you can catch up with us later." The grubber darted off and was quickly lost from sight among the tall grass.

"I did not really believe it when you told me he was as smart as any human," said tiLammis, looking in the direction Reepah had gone, "but now that I know him, I know it is true. I used to think that people were the only intelligent creatures in the world, but now I know of reen and grubbers. I wonder if there are any others?"

"There may be," said Armindor. "There are many parts of the world where no human has set foot since the time of the Fire from the Sky. Who knows what may dwell in them?"

"Nothing else like the reen, I hope," declared the young merchant. "I have been troubled since you told me they were probably living in Ingarron as they lived in Orrello. I pray to Garmood that what happened in Orrello hasn't happened there, too!"

"And I have been praying to Roodemiss for the same thing," said Armindor.

Tigg turned thoughtful eyes upon the magician. "But what if it *has* happened, Armindor? What if we're too late with our warning? What will we do? We can't just give up."

Armindor smiled and reached out to ruffle his apprentice's already touseled hair. "We won't give up, Tigg. If Ingarron has fallen you and Jilla and I shall go on to one of the other southern or western cities, such as Ghay or Preelo, in hope of warning the people there in time. It would be another long, hard journey, but we have become good journeyers by now, eh?"

"It is most fortunate that you are journeying back home at this time," declared tiLammis, who now knew the story of all their adventures. "I see the hands of the gods and spirits in it! No one in this part of the world but you three and the grubber would know how to guard against the reen. Even if I could have lived to make it home, I could only have told the leaders of Ingarron about what happened in Orrello, but I wouldn't have known that Ingarron faced the same danger."

"It is also fortunate that we encountered you," Armindor pointed out. "Not only because we saved you from death, but because your report of what happened in Orrello will make the Ingarronian leaders more heedful of our advice. We have found that great nobles and leaders are not always as wise and reasonable as they ought to be!"

When twilight settled over the meadowland they camped for the night by the side of the trail. Inasmuch as Reepah had not been on hand to forage for them throughout most of the day they faced a supperless evening, but Tigg and Jilla carefully examined the ground around the campsite for a time, to see if they could find any of the edible plants the grubber located so easily.

"Look," said Jilla suddenly, pointing. In the distance they could see a crowd of small figures moving steadily along the trail toward them.

"Grubbers," said Tigg. "Reepah must be bringing his folk to meet us."

It was indeed Reepah and some twenty other grubbers, all carrying spears and bulging sacks made of woven, dried plant fronds. They gathered around the four humans, eyeing them with friendly curiosity. "Tick, my people wish to honor you and Aminda for the saving of me," Reepah announced. "We have brought food for a feast."

And a feast there was. The grubbers had brought flat cakes of baked grain, which they smeared with honey; dried vegetables from which a tasty, filling stew was quickly prepared; and clay pots of a kind of sweet cordial made from fermented berry juice. The humans, who had not eaten so well for nearly a moon, gorged themselves, but so did the little furry creatures, who looked reasonably well fed to begin with.

"Is this your whole community, Reepah?" asked Jilla.

"No, no. These are only the warriors who have akreed to come with us to Inkarron to help fight the reen," the grubber told her.

"What's that—they're all going to help us?" asked Armindor with delight in his voice.

"Yes," Reepah said, turning to him. "I told my people of everything, Aminda—of how the hyoo-mens and reen are at war akainst each other. All my people have akreed that it would be wise for us to help the hyoo-mens in this war, for if the reen should win, they will next come akainst us weenitok. So, most of our young males and females have come to do what they can."

"They are most welcome!" cried the magician. "This is great news, Reepah. With your people's knowledge of the enemy, and your marvelous noses that can smell the creatures out for us, you'll be a powerful weapon in the war against the reen!"

···5···

The next day they began to move through farmland that had been plowed out of the meadow many generations before, and for the following two days they passed through fields of young spring crops and caught frequent sight of farmers' dwellings. By the twentieth day of their journey on the road they could clearly make out the city wall and the rooftops of distant Ingarron.

"No smoke. No sign of damage or trouble," observed Tigg. "Everything seems to be all right."

"Thanks be to Roodemiss," murmured Armindor.

One of the grubbers marching along behind them squeaked out something in its chittering language to Reepah, perched on Tigg's shoulder, who squeaked back an answer, then leaned out toward Armindor. "Aminda, the warriors will ko no farther with us, now. They do not wish to enter the bick community of hyoo-mens until they are sure they will be well treated. They will camp out here and come inside when I can return to tell them all is well."

"That's probably best," Armindor agreed. "The sight of a grubber army marching unannounced through the city gate might cause quite a stir!"

And so the four humans, with Reepah on the boy's shoulder and the hornbeast led by tiLammis, went on alone. By late afternoon they were passing through the city's northern gate and being eyed by lounging guardian Peacekeepers. Tigg was rather surprised to find that he was excited to be back in his native city. Most of his life in Ingarron had not been particularly happy; he had been a ragged, homeless orphan, living by his wits and skill as a thief, pickpocket, and beggar, until Armindor had adopted him and made him an apprentice sage. His sharpest memories were of hunger, discomfort, and fear of being captured by slavers or seized by Peacekeepers, who would have cut off his thumbs to keep him from picking any more pockets. Yet, at the sight of the thatched-roofed, gray log houses lining the street, and the familiar view of the tall gray tower of the house of worship of the god Garmood, the highest structure in the city, Tigg felt a deep sense of satisfaction and pleasure. He was *home!*

To Jilla, Ingarron seemed a strange, exotic place. The northern communities of the Land of Wemms, and the port city of Inbal, with which she was familiar, were nothing like it. The buildings had an odd, bulky look; unfamiliar spicy odors confronted her nose; and although she had grown quite used to the twanging southern accent of Tigg and Armindor, to hear *everyone* in the street speaking in a similar way seemed strange. However, Jilla had never had a really permanent home in all her life—her "home" had been the traveling wagon of her uncle and aunts, the puppeteers—and as she took in the sights, sounds, and smells of Ingarron, the thought that it would be her home from now on excited her.

At the first street intersection, tiLammis halted. "I must go and make a report to my uncle, right away," he said. "Once again, I thank you all most gratefully for saving my life, and I will do whatever I can to help you with your mission to warn our city of the danger of the reen. If you need me for anything, just send word to the Pynjo Merchandising Company." He began to unload the hornbeast, handing the sacks of their belongings to his three companions.

"Please tell your uncle that I am going to order a convocation of all the city's sages for the day after tomorrow, at the Sages' Guildhall, to discuss how to deal with the reen," Armindor told him. "Word will be sent to all the city's leaders to attend, and it would be most helpful for your uncle and the other Master Merchants to be there. I would like to have you there, too, tiLammis, to describe how the reen took over Orrello."

"I will be there," the young man promised, "and I'll urge my uncle to attend and to tell all the other Masters to attend. Farewell, Your Wisdom. Farewell, Tigg, Jilla, Reepah." He turned away, leading his hornbeast up the side street.

"Where are we going now?" questioned Jilla.

"To the Sages' Guildhall of Ingarron," said Armindor. "You can see it straight ahead."

They continued on along the main street which led from the city gate. Jilla could, indeed, see the guildhall ahead—a large, imposing, round building with a great domed roof. From the center of the roof rose a tall flagpole with a fluttering blue banner bearing the white symbol of the eye of Roodemiss, god of sages. Reaching this building, which was surrounded by a wall of upright logs embedded in the ground, they passed through a gateway formed of two logs supporting a horizontal log, and made their way through a small courtyard to a large, intricately carved wooden door that stood wide open. Entering through the doorway, they came into a spacious, wood-paneled, octagonal room with a doorway in each of its eight walls. In the middle of the room was a wooden bench upon which sat a blue-robed woman, her head down and her hands folded in her lap. As Armindor and his three companions entered she looked up, and at the sight of the blue-robed man her eyes widened and she jumped to her feet.

"High Master Armindor!" she exclaimed. "You have returned safely! Thanks to Roodemiss!" She bowed, touching her forehead with the back of her right hand.

Armindor returned her bow. "Yes, I am back, Sister Glinno. It is good to see you again. Which Master is present today?"

"Master Dalinda, High Master."

Armindor nodded. "I must see him at once. That way, young ones," he said, indicating one of the doorways. As Tigg and Jilla, who was carrying Ree-pah, headed toward it, Armindor bent down to whisper something to Sister Glinno. Her eyes flicked toward the children and she nodded.

"Straight down this corridor," said Armindor, catching up to Tigg and Jilla. They walked down a wide hallway, its walls covered with carved wooden panels, its floor made of flagstones, its length lit by lanterns hanging at intervals from the ceiling. At the end of this corridor was a broad door. They stopped in front of it and Armindor rapped.

"Enter," called a voice from beyond the door.

Armindor pushed open the door and guided the children into a spacious room, the walls of which were entirely covered by shelves filled with books—thick sheaves of cloth squares sewn together along one edge, each square page covered with hand-lettered text. In the center of this room sat a man at a stout wooden table, bent in contemplation over a book. He was a middle-aged man, with a balding head and a beard that was a mixture of brown and gray. His reaction to the sight of Armindor was identical to that of Sister Glinno. "High Master!" he exclaimed, hopping off the stool to bow, his hand to his forehead. "You are back!"

"Yes, back at last, Brother Dalinda."

"And—was your mission a success?" asked the other eagerly.

"More successful than any of us could have dreamed," Armindor assured him. "We found only a few actual spells, but we also found something so wonderful as to be almost unbelievable—something that will actually give us the key to all the magic of the ancient world, Brother! It is a device that teaches the language of the Age of Magic! The brothers and sisters of the Guildhall of Inbal are even now working on a vast project to compile wordbooks for the library of every guildhall in the world." He gestured toward the shelves that lined the walls. "Someday we shall finally be able to read and understand all those spells in the ancient tongue that were so carefully copied down by generation after generation of sages, may Roodemiss bless them!"

"Wonderful," said Dalinda in a near whisper. "Thanks be to Roodemiss!"

"Yes, it is wonderful," Armindor agreed. Then his face took on a serious expression, and he leaned forward across the table, looking straight into the other man's eyes. "But all that must wait for a time, Brother. We bear news that is even more important, concerning the very fate of the human race! When my apprentice and I were in the Wild Lands, where we found the spells, we learned of the existence of a kind of creature that no one had ever known about— ratlike beings that are as intelligent as humans, and that have lived hidden among us in all our cities for years. We learned that it is the intention of these creatures, which call themselves reen, to *wipe us out,* Brother Dalinda, and to take our place in the world! We helped fight a battle against the things when we were in Inbal, and when we left there, the people of the city were making ready to wage all-out war against them. But on our way home we learned that the reen had risen up in Orrello, massacred most everyone there, and burned down the city. And they are here in Ingarron, Brother, and we must act against them quickly! I order that a convocation of sages be called for the day after tomorrow, starting at mid morning here in the guildhall, in the Hall of Discussions. Send word to the Lord Director of the city, to the Lord General of the Peacekeepers, to the high priests and priestesses of every god or spirit that has a house of worship here, and to anyone else who has a voice in the affairs of this city. Make them understand that we will be discussing the life or death of Ingarron, Brother!"

Dalinda's mouth was hanging open in astonishment. "It shall be done as you say, High Master. But—"

There was a light knock at the door. "Enter," called Armindor.

Sister Glinno came into the room. She carried a blue bundle, which she handed to Armindor.

"Ah, thank you," he said. "Stay for a moment please, Sister. I want you and Brother Dalinda to be witnesses."

He turned toward Tigg and Jilla, upon whose shoulder Reepah had chosen to sit at this moment. "I have not yet introduced my companions," said Armindor. He indicated the grubber. "This is Reepah, of the weenitok folk, who are, I have found, our equals in intelligence and many other things as well. He is a true friend, who was of tremendous help to us in our long journey to the Wild Lands and back. We could not have safely returned without his aid."

Next, he indicated Jilla. "This is Jilla, of the northlands. She, too, has been of immense help in our recent adventures. In your presence as witnesses, I now adopt her as my daughter." Jilla beamed at him with shining, joyful eyes. She had never dreamed that Armindor would do such a thing. Now, she was truly part of a family again!

"And this is my apprentice, Tigg," said Armindor, putting a hand on the boy's shoulder. "He has shown himself to be loyal, courageous, and highly intelligent. He saved my life in the Wild Lands, and he saved me from capture by our enemies in Inbal. He is as dear to me as a son. But aside from all that, he has shown that he possesses the mind and talents of a true magician. He has fully mastered the arts of reading and working with numbers, and it was he who solved the uses of several of the spells we found. And so, by my authority as a High Master of the Guild of Sages, I now declare that he has fulfilled his apprenticeship and is worthy to be a Novice Sage and full brother of the Guild." He held out the blue bundle to the boy.

"Tigg, here is your sage's robe. The Guild welcomes you, Brother Tigg."

Master Dalinda raised his hand, palm outward, and inclined his head. "Welcome, Brother."

"Welcome, Brother," said Sister Glinno, also with raised palm and inclined head.

Astonished, Tigg took the robe, staring up at Armindor. When he had been a thief and pickpocket there had never been any thought in his mind of ever being anything but a thief and pickpocket. When Armindor had tricked him into becoming a magician's apprentice, the boy had at first been resentful, with no desire to follow the new path he had been set upon. But gradually, because of Armindor's example, Tigg had become interested in the life of a magician, in the seeking and gaining of knowledge and the unraveling of ancient mysteries. When he had decided to make this his life he had known that someday he would wear the blue robe, as all sages did, but that had seemed far in the future. Now, suddenly and unexpectedly, the day was here. And Tigg realized that he, who only a year ago had been an outsider, a guttersnipe with no hope and no future, was now a respectable and respected member of the kind of people who truly counted for something—those who kept the world in order and balance, who created improvements, who served civilization. People, even those much older than he, would now call *him* "Your Wisdom"! Peacekeepers, who a year ago would have cut off his thumbs, would now treat him with respect.

All other sages would call him "Brother" and regard him as one of them. He had become "someone." And it was all because of the tall, stout man with the fringe of white hair and the kindly, youthful face, who was smiling down at him. Tigg found he could not speak, but his eyes brimmed over and two tears of love and joy wound down his cheeks. Armindor gently patted his shoulder, to show that he understood.

The magician then looked up at Dalinda and Glinno. "Well, I know you have a thousand questions," he said, "but I'm afraid they'll have to wait. We four have just completed a journey of many thousands of paces. We've been hungry, thirsty, wet, cold, and in danger. We've been chased by a swamp monster! Our legs ache from tramping. We're going to spend the rest of this day and all of tomorrow just resting and resting—and eating and eating. We shall see you the day after tomorrow, at the convocation, but now—we're going home!"

··· 6 ···

The Hall of Discussions in the Sages' Guildhall of Ingarron was a very large room with one curved wall that was part of the outer wall of the round building. The inner side of the logs of this wall and those forming the other walls was covered with a thick layer of smooth plaster upon which red and black designs were painted. From the huge wooden rafters of the ceiling hung a score of large, clay lanterns that were the hall's only source of light, for the curved wall was windowless.

Now the lanterns glowed with light, and the Hall of Discussions was packed with people. Nearly half the room was taken up by rank upon rank of blue-robed sages seated on rows of low benches. Most of the other half was filled with a variety of personages seated upon an assortment of stools—a cluster of brown-robed priests of Garmood, each with a pair of ornately carved prayer sticks; a bevy of gray-robed priestesses of the Mother of All; a handful of high-ranking Peacekeepers in ceremonial armor; a collection of Master Merchants in orange and russet smocks; and a scattering of Crafters, Artisans, Builders, and Maintainers, in hues of dark gray and black. At the front of this assemblage, attired in a splendid scarlet smock and wearing his official emblem of rank—a neck chain formed of links of the precious metals iron, copper, silver, and gold—was Lord Director Mogariom, ruler of Ingarron, accompanied by a dozen Councilors who were nearly as splendidly attired.

Novice Sage Tigg sat among his Brothers and Sisters and proudly listened as his beloved master arranged the defense of Ingarron against the reen. Armindor stood in a narrow, open space between the sages on one side and the city leaders on the other. He told the crowd how he and Tigg had first learned of the reen in the Wild Lands, when he had been the captive of several of the creatures and had been saved from death by Tigg, Reepah, and a small army of grubbers who lived in the Wild Lands. He repeated the words of the reen leader, who had boasted of how the reen lived unsuspected among people, spying on them, and revealed the reen plan to rise up someday and massacre all humans. The magician described how the reen of Inbal had tried to steal the ancient spells he and Tigg had brought out of the Wild Lands, and how they had attacked the Sages' Guildhall of Inbal. He read the letter from the High Chairman of Inbal, acknowledging the danger of the reen and urging the rulers of all cities to take action against the creatures. He called upon young ti-Lammis, seated with Master Merchant Pynjo, who stood up and described the horror of the reen destruction of Orrello. When the young merchant finished and sat down, Armindor let his gaze rove over the faces of the city leaders of Ingarron, who appeared stunned at what they had heard.

"The creatures are here in Ingarron, too, you may be sure," he told them. "They might rise up as they did in Orrello at any moment. We have to begin *now* to work to prevent that uprising! The reen can be fought and they can be beaten, as they were in Inbal, but we cannot discuss, we cannot argue, we cannot leave things to someone else to do—we must act *at once* and all together, or we will have no chance against them!"

In the silence that followed his words, he again scanned the faces of his audience, as did Tigg. The same thought was in both their minds—is there a traitor here, as there was in Inbal? Will someone now stand up and try to make light of all this, and cast doubt on it, so that nothing will get done and the reen will be able to carry out their plan?

But the first person to stand up was Lord Director Mogariom. He was a man in his early thirties, with a handsome face and an air of self-assurance. Like most Ingarronians he had tan skin and dark eyes, and his hair and beard were lustrous inky-black. For the occasion, he was wearing wooden earrings and a nose plug that were dyed with the red and black colors of Ingarron.

"High Master Armindor," he said in a deep, resonant voice, "you give us a frightening picture, and one that I, and, I suspect, all these others, was not in the least prepared for. Yesterday, everything was peaceful and serene in Ingarron, but now today we find that we have a terrible secret enemy among us, and must make ready for all-out war! This is not a thing that a city ruler does happily, but from what you have told us, and from what Merchant tiLammis tells us of the fate of Orrello, I feel we have no choice." He glanced about at his Councilors, seated around him. "Does my Council agree?"

Tigg held his breath. It had been in a convocation just like this in Inbal, when the traitorous Councilor Leayzar had stood up and managed to persuade everyone to disbelieve in the danger. But there was a general murmur of assent from the Councilors, which was echoed among the others seated in that half of the chamber. "Very well, then," said Mogariom. "High Master Armindor, tell us what we can do to save Ingarron from these things."

Tigg offered a quick, silent prayer of thanks to Roodemiss. This was the best possible result of the meeting. He knew that Armindor had given a great deal of thought on how to act against the threat of the reen, and now the magician was in a position to be able to steer things in the right direction.

"First," said Armindor, "we must keep secret everything that we do, for as I have told you, the reen are constantly spying on human affairs, and if they learn we are preparing against them, they may launch their attack before we can be ready. Early this morning, a number of other sages and I went over every finger width of this room and the adjoining rooms to make sure there was no place where a reen might hide and listen to us. We examined the walls, floors, and ceilings, and I can assure you that no one but those of us in this room knows what goes on here. *And it must remain that way!* Do not tell anyone else, not even your wives, husbands, or children, of what we do. The purpose of this meeting must be kept secret!"

One of the Councilors, a small, sharp-faced man, spoke up. "But many people other than those here know that this meeting was held, and will wonder what it was about. And a secret that is too much of a secret can call attention to itself. I suggest we make up some false reason for holding this meeting, and offer that to anyone who asks, to lull their curiosity rather than increase it."

Roodemiss preserve us from the tricky minds of politicians, thought Armindor. But he had to admit that the idea was probably a good one. "You are right, Councilor," he acknowledged. He thought rapidly, then continued: "Well, many people have now heard that Orrello has been destroyed, although they don't know what truly happened there, and wild rumors are flying. Let us say that we received definite word that Orrello was sacked and burned by an army of marauding barbarians from out of the west, and we met to discuss ways of safeguarding Ingarron from attack by them if they should move down against us. That will also help explain a number of things we'll have to do that we just won't be able to keep secret, such as strengthening the Peacekeeper force."

"It will be well and good to strengthen our force to fight these reen," said the Lord General of the Peacekeepers, a brawny, dark-skinned man, "but what about these poisoned weapons of theirs? How can my men and women protect themselves against those things?"

"With armor," Armindor told him. "The poisoned darts that the reen blow out of their tubes are tiny and fragile, and good stiff leather or wood or animal horn will stop them easily; we learned that in Inbal. Put your people into long-sleeved coats of armor and good thick boots and visored helmets."

"We don't have enough of such equipment, especially if we're going to add people to the force," objected the Peacekeeper Supply Officer, seated beside the Lord General.

"Hire every armorer and leathermaker in the city to produce what you need," said Armindor. "Use the story of the barbarian marauders as your reason for needing such a vast amount of armor so quickly."

"That will cost a great deal of money," observed Lord Director Mogariom, to no one in particular.

"Raise taxes," said the sharp-faced Councilor. "Proclaim a temporary defense tax for the safety of the city. You can always remove it later—perhaps."

And so the talk went on. Ideas flowed from all parts of the room. Armindor urged the sages to put all their thoughts to ways of fighting the reen, and they began to whisper among themselves. The merchants were discussing ways of protecting food supplies, and the Councilors were discussing ways of fighting any fires the reen might start. The Peacekeepers were talking animatedly among themselves, and the Lord General looked up and called to Armindor.

"High Master, we feel we simply cannot wait for these creatures to make their uprising. We must attack *them,* wipe out as many as we can with a quick first move, and put them on the defensive. But you say they live in the sewers and tunnels underneath the city, so how in Maldum's name are we going to get at them?"

Armindor nodded. "My app—that is, my former apprentice, Novice Sage Tigg, and I have discussed that. He thinks he knows of a way. We are going to make sure it is possible, and in a day or two we shall explain it to you." He turned and looked at Tigg, who stood up and slipped out of the room.

Tigg made his way down a long hall, his sandals slapping on the flagstone floor. He had never worn sandals before, but now that he was a sage he could no longer go barefoot as most ordinary people did. He passed through the octagonal entrance chamber, where an elderly sage acting as doorkeeper for the day sat dozing on the bench, and left the building. Near the entrance, in the small courtyard within the log wall that surrounded the guildhall, Jilla sat cross-legged on the ground, playing the game of Palm, Fist, and Fingers with Reepah, who squatted opposite her. There had been no legitimate way for Jilla to attend the high-level meeting taking place in the guildhall, but she had wanted to stay as near to Tigg and Armindor as she could, and Reepah had elected to stay with her. She glanced up and, seeing Tigg, smiled. The sunlight made her hair the color of red gold.

"How are things going?" she asked.

"Fine," he answered, halting before her. "Everything is happening just as Armindor hoped it would. I'm off now to see if I can get that idea of mine to work."

Jilla nodded. She smiled again. "You look nice in your robe, Tigg."

Tigg was surprised to feel himself grow warm with embarrassment. "Thanks," he mumbled. "I'll see you again soon." He hurried off.

He quickly made his way into the heart of the city, into an area where old, shabby houses were thickly crowded together, and where the smocks and dresses of the men and women he passed on the streets were noticeably ragged, patched, and soiled. The air was thick with a mixture of the smells of cooking spices, garbage, and dung, and there was a kind of subdued noisiness everywhere. This was the "oldtown," a part of Ingarron where "respectable" people seldom came, and the sight of the young sage caused many a curious glance. There would have been danger here for any ordinary youth or child, but Tigg knew that his blue robe was protection against slavers, robbers, ruffians, and any others for whom an ordinary young boy might have been fair game. No one would dare lay a hand on a sage, for most people believed that sages had the power to deliver curses that would bring bad luck, disease, or even violent death.

Tigg was also protected by his manner, for he moved with a self-assurance and purposefulness that seemed to indicate complete confidence in his ability to take care of himself. The fact was, he was not in the least bit afraid to be in this place, for this was where he had lived and grown up before joining Armindor, and he was fully familiar with every nook and cranny of it, as well as with its inhabitants. He passed a pair of ragged urchins, a year or so younger than he, who eyed him with interest and commented on his appearance. "A yont slight for a bluer, nyeh?" said one, and, "Uhs, a mere cubber," replied the other. They were speaking street lango, a kind of secret dialect used by thieves, criminals, and the lowest class of Ingarron's citizenry, and Tigg's lips twitched in a smile, because he understood them perfectly; he had grown up speaking the same cant. One boy had said, "He's a bit small for a sage, isn't he?," and the other had answered, "Yes, he's just a kid." As a matter of fact, Tigg knew both the boys, who were pickpockets as he had been, although they obviously didn't recognize him. He considered, for a moment, surprising them by speaking out in lango and revealing who he was, but quickly decided that might not be wise.

He continued on through the narrow, dingy, smelly streets, making his way toward a large building that loomed over all its neighbors. It had once been a house of worship of a little-known god with few followers who finally all died out, leaving the place abandoned. It had stood empty for a number of years, then had been taken over by a group of people whose leader was the person Tigg had come into this part of the city to see. The entrance to the building stood open, but a man was lounging beside it, arms folded, one leg crossed over the other, shoulders resting against the thick, gray log that formed part of the door frame. He was a burly young man, and Tigg knew that despite his appearance of nonchalance, he was a guard, stationed here to keep unwanted intruders from entering the building. While Tigg might have simply taken advantage of his blue robe to walk past the man unchallenged, such an action would not have been respectful to the person he had come to see. So the boy halted a few paces from the entrance and stood, hands folded over his belly and tucked into the sleeves of his robe, in a position of patient waiting.

The guard eyed the small, robed and sandaled figure with the same curiosity everyone else in the area had displayed at the sight of him, but the man was aware that Tigg wanted something of him. "Can I do something for you, Your Wisdom?" he asked. "Are you lost? Need directions for getting out of this part of town?"

Tigg shook his head. "I know where I am," he told the man. "I have come to speak with the King of the Ratcatchers."

7

The guard stared in surprise. "What do you know of the Ratcatchers? Who told you of us?" he demanded. He was astonished that someone from the "respectable" regions of the city would know of the existence of something that was part of the furtive, underground life of the ghetto.

Long ago, Armindor had taught Tigg a simple secret known to all sages, a secret that helped keep sages feared and respected by other people. If you know something that someone else does not know, Armindor had explained, make it seem that you have that knowledge only because you are a sage—make it seem like magic. Tigg now used his knowledge of the Ratcatchers, gained from his days as a ghetto pickpocket, to impress the guard.

"No one had to tell me anything," he said, looking the man straight in the eye. "I am a sage, and what I wish to know, I have the power to find out. I know that the Ratcatchers are a guild, formed of twenty-eight families whose sons are reared to be Ratcatchers and whose daughters are reared to be the wives of Ratcatchers. No one not born into a Ratcatcher family can ever become a Ratcatcher, and no one born a Ratcatcher can ever become anything else. I know that the Ratcatchers are the providers of the only kind of meat that the poor of Ingarron can afford. I know that you hunt your prey in the sewers and tunnels beneath the city. I know that you have a king whose name is Goorm. I have come to see him." He was gambling that the leader of the Ratcatchers was the same man who had been in charge a year ago.

The guard *was* impressed. None of the people of the area would have told this young sage any of these things; clearly, he did, indeed, have power! "Come with me, Your Wisdom," said the man in a respectful tone. "I'll take you to King Goorm."

Tigg followed him into the building. Most of the interior was a single large hall capable of holding the scores of worshipers that had once come together here to conduct the ceremonies that honored their god. The place was feebly illuminated by dingy light that filtered down through a large, square skylight in the ceiling. The skylight contained a mosaic pattern of wooden strips into which paper-thin pieces of animal horn were fitted. In the dim light Tigg could see that the plastered walls were covered with peeling and faded paintings of scenes that must have been of significance to the religion practiced here; he could make out many figures of kneeling people and what seemed to be winged, robed forms flying in the sky, all gazing toward a single gleaming, metallic-looking figure standing in the midst of a mushroom-shaped burst of radiance. The boy wondered, for a moment, what sort of god or spirit had been worshiped here that was now so completely forgotten. What had happened to that god? Did a god *die* when it was no longer worshiped by anyone?

At the far end of the large hall was a door, toward which the guard headed. Halting before it, the man knocked four times.

"What is it?" called a voice.

"You have, uh, a visitor, sir," said the guard.

"All right, bring whoever it is in."

The guard opened the door and preceded Tigg into the room. It was a small room that had probably once been a priest's study; there were shelves along one wall and a large table, at which a man sat working with a counting board and making tally marks with a charcoal stick on a square of cloth. He was a big man, probably in his early forties, with a nose like a bird of prey's beak and a zig zag scar that puckered one cheek. He wore earrings that were fashioned from tiny, white bones, and instead of a cloth smock he was garbed in a sleeveless garment of varying shades of gray and brown, which Tigg recognized as being made of the pelts of many rats, sewn together. The man gave Tigg a surprised glance then turned to look at the guard with a frown.

"He knows all about us, sir," the guard explained,

as if defending his decision to have brought Tigg here. "He asked for you by name!"

Tigg stepped forward. "I am Novice Sage Tigg. I bring you a message from Armindor, High Master of the Sages, and Mogariom, Lord Director of the city."

The man who called himself the King of the Rat-catchers raised his eyebrows. "My, my. And what do such lofty persons have to say to the likes of me?" he asked in a soft voice that held a faint sneer.

"They ask your help, to save the lives of all your people and of everyone else in the city of Ingarron!"

Goorm frowned. "Explain."

Tigg leaned toward him over the table, lowering his voice. For all he knew there was a reen hiding behind one of the walls, spying on them this very moment. "Have you heard what has happened to Orrello?"

"Why, I have heard that Orrello has burnt to the ground and most of its people have perished," said Goorm. "A terrible catastrophe, but fires will happen. What has this to do with Ingarron?"

"The fire that destroyed Orrello did not happen by accident," Tigg told him. "Orrello was attacked from within by creatures that lived underground in the city's sewers. They wiped out most of the people and set the city afire. They resemble rats, but they have the intelligence of humans. They are—"

But Goorm interrupted him. The man's eyes flicked to look at the young guard. "Them!" he said, in a voice thick with hate. The guard nodded, his mouth a grim line.

Tigg could not hide his surprise. "You know of them?"

Goorm looked back at him. "Oh, yes, we know of them, Your Wisdom. Ratcatchers have been going down into the city's sewers for many generations, and we realized long ago that something was down there that watched us with hatred. We learned that there are parts of the underground where it is death to go; many Ratcatchers vanished forever in those parts, and others were found lying dead on the edge of them. Nearly a hundred summers ago, a war party went into one of those sections to find and wipe out whatever it was that was in them. Of some thirty men that went, only two returned, and they told of ratlike things that wore clothing and attacked the war party with strange, deadly weapons. In the years since, more and more sections of the sewers and tunnels have been closed off to us, and when a man goes down below now, to set his traps or gather up his catches, he knows he risks death! There is hardly a Ratcatcher family that has not lost at least one of its members to the poisoned darts of the god-cursed things!" He rubbed his smooth-shaven chin in a gesture of obvious agitation. "But it never occurred to any of us that the same kinds of creatures might be living under another city as well as this one. And who could have dreamed that they would be able to destroy an entire city!"

"They have been living in all our communities and spying on us for generations," Tigg told him. The boy was elated to find that the Ratcatchers knew of the reen; he had expected to have to convince them that such creatures existed. "But they do not intend to stay in the sewers forever. They have a plan. What they did in Orrello, they intend to do everywhere. They want to wipe all humans off the face of the earth and make the world their own!"

The guard sucked in his breath in a startled hiss, but Goorm merely nodded. "And the ones living beneath Ingarron are going to try to destroy this city soon—that is what the message to me means, does it not? But why especially ask for *our* help?"

"Because," said Tigg, "we are not going to wait for them to attack. We are going down into the sewers to attack *them*. That is why we want your help. We need guides, to lead our war parties through the sewers. Who could do that better than Ratcatchers?"

"Huh! You want us to lead you to your death and ours. Your war parties will be massacred just as the war party our forefathers sent against them was massacred," Goorm bleakly predicted.

Tigg shook his head. "No. The Peacekeepers will be heavily armored, with armor that reen darts can't penetrate."

The Ratcatcher leader looked thoughtful. "That would make a difference," he admitted. He leaned forward. "But the creatures control many hundreds of paces of sewer. We could guide you into their tunnels, yes, but then the things would probably just scatter, and your soldiers could spend days fruitlessly searching for them. We think that somewhere in the tunnels they control there is a kind of city, or community, where they congregate. If you could find exactly where that is, and launch your attack at it—"

"We can find where it is," said Tigg. "We have a way." He was thinking of the marvelous noses of the grubbers, but Goorm eyed him respectfully, thinking he meant some kind of magic. The man nodded slowly.

"In that case, young sage, I think we might well be willing to give the help that's needed. It would certainly be of great value to us if our enemies could be eliminated, and it would be sweet vengeance to help eliminate them! It would also, of course, be to our benefit to help keep the god-cursed things from destroying our city! When do you plan to make your attack on them?"

Tigg grinned. "That was to depend on whether or not I was able to gain your help, King Goorm. Now that I have gained it, I can promise you that the attack will be made soon. I will visit you again in a day or so and tell you everything you'll need to know." He paused, then said earnestly, "All this must be kept secret, of course. No word of what I have told you can be allowed to leak out among other people lest the reen—the ratlike creatures—learn what we intend."

"Have no fear," said Goorm. "Very well then, Your Wisdom, I'll expect to see you again in a day or two. And you may tell the High Master and the Lord Director that when the time comes, they will be able to count on the Ratcatchers."

··· 8 ···

In the days following the convocation at the Sages' Guildhall, preparations for the war against the reen went on at a feverish pace. Heralds on hornbeasts rode through the streets calling for "young and sturdy" volunteers to join the Peacekeepers and help defend the city against the possible onslaught of the western barbarians who had destroyed Orrello. Every leather tanner in Ingarron had his entire stock of cured hides bought up by servants of the Lord Director, who did not blink at paying the highest prices quoted. Every one of the city's leather-fashioners was visited by the Peacekeeper Supply Officer and given orders for large quantities of armor, helmets, armored breeches, and thick boots, to be delivered as soon as possible, and to be made from leather furnished by the Lord Director at moderate prices. The artisans who made necklaces, windowpanes, knife hilts, and other items out of animal horn were suddenly swamped with orders for thick circles and rectangles of the sort that were sewn onto leather coats to make armor. Stonecutters noticed an increase in orders for spearheads, and woodcarvers began to receive many orders for a peculiar sort of flat-sided club that the Peacekeepers wanted for some reason. Thus, business began to boom for all these craftsmen and manufacturers, and they rejoiced—until, like everyone else, they were visited by agents of the Lord Director's Tax Gatherer, who announced the levying of a special new "defense tax" on all the city's citizens.

Within the big, walled enclosure that surrounded the Peacekeepers' barracks and headquarters, new recruits and old veterans trained and trained and trained, learning to move in close-packed rows, their bodies bent forward, stamping down hard with each step, and flailing downward with the special clubs they had been issued, as if to smash and batter opponents that were close to the ground. "Those western barbarians must be dwarfs," they speculated, wondering at these odd tactics. But they were ordered not to discuss this new kind of training with anyone, at the risk of being punished with a whipping if they did so.

Armindor's request to the sages to bend their thoughts to ways of fighting the reen brought results almost at once. A young woman sage, Nallo by name, came to him in the Chamber of Demonstration at the guildhall and presented an idea.

"My field of study is fire and the substances that contain fire," she told him. "I have discovered something that might be a useful weapon against the rat creatures, High Master."

She had brought a number of things with her: a clay dish, a clay bottle, and a bit of twisted cloth that reeked of a pungent odor. Placing the dish on one of the stone tables that stood in the chamber, she poured a small quantity of clear, oily liquid into it from the bottle. Picking up a nearby candle in its holder, she touched the burning wick to the liquid in the dish. The liquid became a pool of flame that sent coils of black smoke swirling toward the ceiling. A sharp smell filled the air.

"Interesting," said Armindor. "What is the liquid, Sister?"

"Several thousand paces south of the city, near the border of the Yellow Desert, there is a place where thick, black, greasy stuff seeps up out of the ground," she told him. "I discovered that it burns just as rendered animal fat or palm oil does. I put some through the Spell of Clearing a Liquid—you know, the process in which you heat a liquid in a flask and let the steam flow through a long tube into another flask, where it becomes a liquid again—and got this clear liquid that burns even better than the black stuff. I found that cloth that is soaked with the clear liquid burns quickly and easily." She placed the bit of twisted cloth in the dish, where the liquid had all burned away, and touched the candle flame to it. It burned vigorously and steadily.

"My idea is this, High Master," she said, looking at him intently. "Fill bottles with the liquid and seal them shut with wads of cloth that have been soaked in the liquid. If you set fire to the cloth and then *throw* the bottle, it breaks and the liquid in it catches fire from the burning cloth and makes a big, flaming puddle on the ground. I've tried this out. It seems to me that if you threw such bottles into crowds of the rat creatures, a lot of them would be splashed with burning liquid and would be too hurt and terrified to do anything but run away! It would eliminate whole groups of them all at once, whereas you can only eliminate one at a time with a club or spear."

"I think you are quite right," Armindor agreed. "It should be an excellent weapon against them. And apart from that, Sister, your work with this fire liquid is quite commendable. What is your rank?"

"I am a Junior Sage, High Master."

"From now on you're a Senior Sage," he told her.

Under Senior Sage Nallo's direction, quantities of "fire bottles" were prepared. Several were tried out on the drill field of the Peacekeepers, so that the soldiers could see how to use them.

"That ought to singe the reens' cursed little furry feet," growled the Lord General of the Peacekeepers, watching the tests of the fire bottles. "Well, I think we're all ready now, High Master Armindor. It's time to put those grubber friends of yours to work to locate the enemy."

Early on the following morning, a small procession made its way out of the city's north gate and headed into the countryside. The procession consisted of Tigg, Jilla, and a score of nondescript-appearing young men and women who were actually Peacekeepers without their armor on. Everyone carried a large, loosely woven wicker basket, and Reepah rode on Tigg's shoulder. Anyone seeing them go—human or reen—would have given them little attention, merely assuming that some wealthy noble or merchant was planning a feast and had sent his servants out into the farm area to bring back baskets of provisions.

After a short march along the road that ran through fields of ripening farm crops, Reepah instructed Tigg to halt. "I will ko and tell the warriors what they must do," he said, "then I will bring them back here."

He moved out of sight among the tall plants in a nearby field, and a short time later returned at the head of the group of grubbers that had volunteered to come and help fight the reen in Ingarron. They showed some nervousness at the presence of so many humans, but the Peacekeepers had been instructed to treat them with care and respect, and Reepah had assured his tribe-members that they would be safe and well treated. The Peacekeepers put their baskets on the ground, a grubber climbed into each and made itself comfortable, the covers were replaced on the baskets, and the procession made its way back to Ingarron.

"All right," said Tigg in a low voice as they reached the city gate. "You know what to do. May luck and your gods be with you."

The group broke up, each person turning onto a

different street, carrying his or her basket. Each Peacekeeper had been assigned a section of the city to walk through slowly while his or her accompanying grubber, in its basket, sniffed for the telltale odors that would reveal where the reen community was located beneath the streets. When one of the grubbers detected the reen center, it was to call out a single word in its own language, which each Peacekeeper had been taught to recognize. The Peacekeeper would then hurry to a central location, the worship house of Garmood, where Armindor, the Lord General, and other officials were waiting, and report where the reen community had been found. A signal, the booming of the huge drum at Peacekeeper headquarters, which was used for alerting Peacekeepers and could be heard throughout the city, would then call all the other teams of Peacekeepers and grubbers off the search.

Tigg and Reepah had also been assigned to check a part of the city, the section that included the worship house of Garmood. Carrying the basket in which Reepah rode, and accompanied by Jilla, the young sage walked slowly up one street and down another.

"You once told me that a city was filled with the smell of reen, Reepah," said Jilla, bending toward the basket so the grubber could hear her. "How will you be able to tell where their gathering place is?"

"It will be a bik, bik, ukly smell," came the grubber's voice. "I will know!"

They had covered most of the section they were to

search without Reepah detecting anything, when the booming of the Peacekeeper signal drum suddenly resounded through the city. "They've found it," exulted Tigg. "Come on!"

Only a few days before he would have sped through the streets on twinkling feet, but now, mindful of his dignity as a blue-robed sage, he limited himself to a brisk walk. Even so, because he and Jilla and Reepah had been so near the house of Garmood to begin with, they were among the first of the search teams to arrive. Just inside the entrance to the tall gray tower, Armindor, the Lord General of the Peacekeepers, and several others were talking with a young woman Peacekeeper whose grubber accomplice had climbed out of its basket and was peering about with interest at the interior of the structure.

"Where is it?" questioned Tigg eagerly.

Armindor told him. The boy's eyes widened, his mouth dropped open, and he began to howl with laughter.

"Why do you laugh?" asked Armindor, looking at him with curiosity.

"I can't wait to see the Ratcatcher king's face when he hears this," gasped Tigg. "The reen city is right under the old, abandoned worship house that Goorm uses as his headquarters!"

· · · 9 · · ·

In the blackness of the middle-night hours of the third day of the Moon of Rains, when most of the honest citizens of Ingarron were fast asleep on their mats, companies of Peacekeepers moved stealthily through the city streets, making their way to the oldtown section where stood the abandoned house of worship that was the headquarters of the Ratcatchers—and beneath which lay the community of the reen. Armindor, the Peacekeeper Lord General, and the others in charge of the war against the reen had not wanted to stir up excitement and apprehension among Ingarron's citizens by the sight of many fully armed and armored Peacekeepers moving purposefully through the city, for this might have drawn the attention of the reen and alerted them to their danger. So it had been decided to make the attack on the reen at night, in as much secrecy as possible. After all, the sewers beneath the city would be no darker then than they were during daylight hours.

A plan had been worked out with the help of

Goorm and some of the other Ratcatchers. The main attack would be made by several companies of Peace-keepers that would be led by a Ratcatcher guide through one of the tunnels that ran to the area where the reen community was located. Meanwhile, other Ratcatchers would guide companies of Peacekeepers into all the other tunnels that led away from the reen community; there the soldiers would be stationed to block the escape of any of the rat-creatures that might try to get away from the area where the main attack was taking place. Armindor and the others hoped that the reen would be caught completely by surprise, and that as many of them as possible might be wiped out and their community destroyed.

It was only a bit earlier this very night that the Peacekeeper soldiers had finally been told who their enemy actually was and what their days of training had been for. Most of them seemed amused that so much effort was being made simply to try to exter-minate what was nothing more than a "smart rat," and felt the attack would be easy and relatively free of danger. A few were resentful that they were being used for such a menial task. "I didn't join the Peace-keepers to hunt rats," they grumbled. "I don't think they should use *us* for this!" But if the soldiers' troop commander overheard such mutterings, the retort was quick and sharp. "You're not paid to *think*, you're paid to do what you're told," the commander would growl. "So shut your mouth and do what you're told!"

The companies of soldiers assembled outside

Goorm's abandoned worship house were assigned their guides, for whom battle armor like that of the soldiers had been provided, and moved off as silently as possible to the places where they would descend into the sewers. "How will we get down there?" the Senior Company Commander, who was to lead the main attack, asked of her guide.

"Right through my house," the man answered. "Every Ratcatcher has an entrance to the underground right in his cellar."

Reaching the man's home, the soldiers filed down a short, narrow flight of stone steps into the cellar, where there was, indeed, a thick, wooden door set into one wall. "All right, light the torches and let's do our job," ordered the commander.

The Ratcatcher slid back the bolts that barred the door and opened it onto pitch blackness. The Peace-keeper soldiers began to move through the doorway, into the realm of the reen.

They went in groups of three; one soldier holding a torch and carrying a quantity of Sister Nallo's fire bottles in a bag slung from his or her shoulder, another clutching a trio of light throwing spears, and the third bearing one of the special flat-headed wooden clubs the Peacekeepers had been practicing with for days. Each trio moved in the formation of a tight triangle, those with spear and club side by side so their bodies and big shields could provide protection for the shieldless light-bearer, who moved right behind them, holding a torch in one hand and keeping the other free to ignite and throw fire bottles when necessary.

"Keep moving straight ahead until I tell you to turn," ordered the Ratcatcher, who was acting as torchbearer for the commander and her assistant commander. The trios of soldiers began to spread out, but kept a distance of only a few paces from one another.

"I had no idea it would be so roomy down here," whispered the Peacekeeper commander. "It's like walking through streets!"

"These *were* streets once," the Ratcatcher told her. "They were the streets of a city that stood here long ago—maybe during the Age of Magic! Ingarron is built right on top of it. We find strange, old objects down here sometimes. Things that were used by the people who lived here thousands of years ago."

The flickering light of several score of torches revealed the strange surroundings through which the companies moved. Long, straight sections of wall rose on each side, formed of what seemed to be a kind of stone, pitted and pocked by centuries of seeping moisture, and blackened and scarred as if once subjected to a titanically hot fire. In places there were large, rectangular openings in the walls that were mostly covered by gray, tattered, curtainlike swaths formed of the cobwebs from thousands of generations of spiders. Through rents and gaps in these gauzy draperies, the torchlight revealed vast, debris-littered interiors. There was an occasional gleam from a tiny shard of the clear glass that the ancients had once manufactured, winking back torchlight from where it lay among the rubble. There was also an occasional large mass of gritty brownish-red, draped with cobwebs, standing near a wall, with an oddly symmetrical look and a suggestion of wheels underneath that hinted it might once have been an artificial object of some unknown use, perhaps a vehicle. The ground underfoot was a powdery rubble, the accumulation of centuries of dust. The air was thick and dank, saturated with an odor of rotting food that had been dragged underground by hordes of rats, the unpleasant tang of mildew, and a general mustiness. Somewhere far in the distance was the steady *ush* of rapidly moving water.

"Turn right, here, and be on your guard," directed the Ratcatcher guide. "We will be entering *their* domain."

The soldiers followed his directions, proceeding cautiously. They had grown used to the sight of the sudden twin gleams of rat eyes staring at them from shadowed crannies, blinking in the torchlight and vanishing as the rat darted off in fright, but now, after a few hundred paces, the lead trio of soldiers encountered two pairs of gleams that did not vanish, and the torchlight revealed two reen crouched beside a large, blocklike chunk of stone. That the creatures were not rats was obvious: they stood upright on two legs, each had what appeared to be a leather bag slung from its shoulder, and each carried a slim blowtube of white bone. One of the creatures raised its tube to its mouth and puffed its cheeks.

"Cover!" shouted the Peacekeeper commander. The soldiers of the lead trio, toward which the reen was aiming, froze in a crouch, and the two front men raised their big shields. In the underground silence, the faint *snick* of the reen dart striking a shield could be clearly heard. A moment later the spearman straightened up, took a quick step forward, and with a snap throw sent one of his spears plunging into the body of the reen that had shot the dart, killing the creature instantly. The second reen spun about and sped out of sight into the darkness.

"They'll know we're coming, now," the Peacekeeper commander remarked to herself. She raised her voice. "Form into line. Proceed with caution, at quick-march pace."

The trios closed together until they formed double rows that stretched from wall to wall of the tunnel, the front of each row made up of alternate spear-carriers and club-wielders, the second row of torch-bearers each a few paces apart. No reen could possibly slip past or through this series of lines. Abandoning stealth, the soldiers moved forward at a steady marching tread.

After a time, they became aware that darts were hissing at them out of the darkness, where reen had gathered to fight off this sudden, unexpected invasion of their territory. But the darts stuck in shields or bounced harmlessly off the thick leather and hard horn of the armor that covered the Peacekeepers' bodies. Even so, there was a sudden crash and clatter of armor and shield as a Peacekeeper in the front row went down, struck by a lucky shot of a dart that came through one of the small openings in his helmet visor and penetrated the skin of his face.

"Leave him!" snapped the Peacekeeper commander, as the soldier on each side of the fallen man hesitated for a moment beside his body. "You can't help him; those darts kill instantly. But that was a lucky shot. They may get a few of us that way, but they can't stop us!"

It was true. The humans could hear sibilant whisperings as the reen spoke to one another, and there was desperation in the hissing voices. The reen realized that their darts were almost useless against the heavily protected humans. They continuously fell back, to stay out of the torchlight, but from time to time one would be a trifle too slow, and a quickly thrown spear would rip into it. Wounded reen, lying in the path of the advancing lines, were dispatched by club-wielding Peacekeepers.

"We should be directly beneath the old worship house in about another hundred paces or so," said the Ratcatcher guide. "If that's where the god-cursed things do have their city, we're nearly there!"

"Hear that, soldiers?" called the commander. "Look sharp!"

The spear-carriers cocked their arms for quick throws, the club-wielders hefted their weapons, the torchbearers slid their free hands into the bags slung from their shoulders and closed them around fire bottles. Suddenly a noise resounded through the tunnel—an excited, high-pitched murmur coming from ahead. The fleeing reen had brought word that human attackers were on the outskirts of the reen community, and the inhabitants were now in a panic.

After some fifty paces, the Peacekeepers suddenly became aware that the tunnel had come to an end and that they were moving into a larger, open area. "Extend line, extend line!" yelled troop commanders, and soldiers at each side of the back rows hurried forward to attach themselves to the ends of the front line in order to lengthen it. There were faint glimmering spots of light in the darkness directly in front of the attackers, but the torchlight did not extend far enough to show what they were advancing into.

"We've got to see better!" said the commander, her voice cracking with anxiety. "Even numbers throw fire!" she yelled.

Alternate torchbearers in the forward row plucked clay bottles out of their bags, stuck the mouths of the bottles into their flaming torches, setting the flammable cloth stoppers ablaze, and flung the bottles out ahead of the advancing line. The bottles arced through the darkness as curving spots of fire. Wherever one of the several dozen missiles struck, there was a sudden splash of flame that quickly spread out in a blazing pool. The dozens of fiery patches provided a dim, lurid glow that revealed what lay in front of the oncoming Peacekeepers. An almost universal exclamation of surprise burst from all the humans at what they saw.

The city of the reen was located in a broad, open area that had once been a small park in the ancient town that lay beneath modern Ingarron. Probably some twenty centuries earlier, the ancestors of the present-day reen had begun building their community, using objects they discovered during their forays into the remains of the buildings that formed the walls of the underground tunnels. And so, the reen city was literally constructed of human *junk*—lengths of plastic siding, chunks of concrete, broken bricks, automobile parts, rust-coated steel doors and shutters, and thousands of rusted cans of all sorts had been piled together to form the dwellings of the reen. But, unlike a human community, there were no streets and individual houses; the reen city was a giant maze of hundreds of adjoining squares and rectangles, like rooms rather than separate dwellings, interconnected by openings in two or more walls. These living spaces were no more than waist-high to a human, and because neither rain nor snow could fall on this underground community, all the dwellings were roofless, and the humans could look right into the nearest ones. The junk forming the walls was held in place by a kind of mortar of mud, clay, and water, and into this, while it was still wet, the reen builders had pressed thousands of fragments of glass and shiny plastic, so that the walls of their living quarters sparkled in the glow of the flaming pools. It was clear that they must have sparkled for the reen at all times, for although the reen were nocturnal creatures, like all nocturnal creatures they needed *some* light with which to see in darkness, and small, oddly shaped oil lamps flickered dimly in most of the dwellings. It was the glow of these that the Peacekeepers had seen as they advanced in darkness toward the reen community.

All this was an alien, exotic sight to the humans, but not one they could spend time staring at. Reen darts by the score were hissing at them from every direction, and another soldier went down, hit by a missile that had slipped through an opening in his visor. The reen had been caught completely by surprise, but they outnumbered the attacking force by hundreds to one, and if they were given time to recover from their shock, they might swarm against the humans and pull them down by sheer weight of numbers. The Peacekeeper commander knew that she had to make the reen so terrorized and desperate that they would lose all thoughts of resistance and seek only to escape.

"Odd numbers throw fire," she screamed. Another barrage of clay bottles arced out toward the reen community and burst into several dozen more fiery patches. The community began to seethe with frantic motion, and its inhabitants' cries rose to a steady shriek. Scores of the reen, splashed by the flaming liquid, sought to escape their agony by clawing and pummeling a path through any other reen in their way. Many of those that had been blowing darts at the attackers were now forced out of their positions by spreading fire, and the swarm of darts that had been sailing at the Peacekeepers dwindled to only a few.

"Advance in line," shrilled the Peacekeeper commander. "Smash 'em!"

The front row of spear- and club-bearing soldiers, with shields lifted and bodies bent in a crouch, moved forward with the stomping tread they had been practicing for days. The first row of fire-bottle throwers marched behind them, their eyes darting about for possible targets. Following them came more alternate rows of spear- and club-bearers and fire-bottle bearers, as the entire Peacekeeper force, nearly a hundred strong, launched its attack.

Reaching the nearest reen dwellings, the men and women clambered over the walls. Here and there along the line soldiers stabbed with spears and flailed with clubs as they encountered reen that had been cut off from escape, that were trying to hide, or that had even turned to fight.

"Throw fire at will," ordered the commander.

A fire bottle burst into flames among a group of reen shooting darts from behind a wall, and they scattered, flinging down their weapons and shrieking with pain. Dozens of bottles burst among the thick crowd of rat-creatures trying to flee into the far corners of the community. A stench like the odor of burning meat filled the air, and the ear-splitting shrieks of thousands of reen rang through the tunnel.

The Peacekeeper units that had been stationed in the other tunnels leading to the reen community heard the din and knew the attack was under way. "Move forward slowly," their commanders ordered, and each company, formed into alternate lines of spear- and club-bearers and fire-bottle throwers that stretched from wall to wall across the tunnel, stepped off in a slow tread. They began to encounter groups of reen fleeing from the reen community. The creatures shrieked in terror at the sight of the long line of human soldiers and the realization that their escape was cut off. Fire bottles burst among them, and some of the creatures turned and fled back the way they had come, while others desperately tried to push and claw their way through the legs of the advancing Peacekeepers. They were speared and clubbed to death.

Slowly, the Peacekeeper companies in each tunnel converged on the open area where the reen community was located, slaughtering crowds of reen as they came. The noise of the rat-creatures' shrieks gradually diminished, and by the time all the human soldiers had gathered among the glittering walls of the community there was near silence except for the sounds of human movements and human voices. The Peacekeeper Lord General, who had accompanied one of the units that had come through an adjoining tunnel, stood with his hands on his hips and his legs widespread, peering about in satisfaction. The clustered torches lit up the area almost as brightly as daylight and revealed the crumpled bodies of hundreds of the rat-creatures, sprawled in the interconnected squares and rectangles of the reen community. Scores of more dead reen lay in each of the tunnels through which a Peacekeeper company had come.

The general nodded to himself. "All right," he said. "We've taken care of them. They won't be any trouble to us now!"

· · · 10 · · ·

The people of Ingarron were awakened at first light the next morning by the booming of drums and the blaring of the huge wooden alarm-horns mounted on the city walls—sounds that were heard together only rarely and that indicated some special event. People hurried from their homes and stood sleepy-eyed in the streets, wondering what had happened. Was there a fire? Was the city being attacked? Had the Lord Director died?

Heralds on hornbeasts began to appear in all the main streets, calling out the news. They were eager to proclaim a great victory for the people of Ingarron and embellished their reports accordingly. A terrible danger to the city had been averted, they announced, thanks to the quick efforts of the Lord Director. It had been discovered that a hitherto unknown race of intelligent, ratlike creatures was living in the tunnels and sewers beneath Ingarron. Creatures such as these had actually caused the destruction of Orrello, and they had planned to destroy Ingarron as well. But during the night the city's brave Peacekeepers had fought a battle against the creatures, killing thousands of them and driving the rest out of the city. Ingarron was now safe, and the Lord Director declared a holiday of thanksgiving and celebration. Barrels of beer and berry wine would be opened in the main square, and free beer and wine would be dispensed to Ingarron's citizens all day long, thanks to the Lord Director.

Those who didn't hear this news from the heralds soon heard it from friends or neighbors, and by the time the sun was no more than three finger widths above the horizon almost everyone in Ingarron knew what had happened and was prepared to join the celebration. Many people put on their feast-day finery, earrings, nose plugs, and wrist and ankle bracelets, and headed for the main square and the free drinks. Jugglers, clowns, acrobats, musicians, puppeteers, and peddlers headed there also, as did the city's pickpockets and beggars, all intent on making as much money as they possibly could out of the huge, good-natured crowd that would be present. Ingarron gave itself over to a day of fun and feasting.

"I don't like it," said Armindor.

He had been up since long before dawn, when he had been awakened to hear a report by a Peacekeeper officer on the outcome of the underground battle. With Tigg and Jilla, he had hurried to the site of the battle to look things over. Now it was midday, and the three of them stood with Goorm and several other

Ratcatchers, gazing at the strange sight of the reen community. Torches had been stuck wherever they would stand upright, and the place blazed with light. A number of Peacekeepers moved slowly about among the maze of reen dwellings, searching for any reen bodies that might have been overlooked up to now. Fearful of the danger of disease from rotting corpses beneath the city, Armindor had ordered that all the dead reen be disposed of, and since early morning, Peacekeepers had been collecting reen bodies and stuffing them into bags which were then piled on squnt-drawn wagons and taken to the burial grounds far outside the city. There they were soaked with Sister Nallo's flammable oil, at Armindor's suggestion, and burnt. Few Peacekeepers could count much higher than ten, but Armindor had instructed them to put five bodies in each bag, and by keeping a tally of the bags, he and Tigg had determined that just about 315 reen had been killed.

"I don't like it," said Armindor, when it became obvious that all the bodies had been found and the count was finished. "Only three hundred and fifteen reen dead? From what we know of them, there must have been thousands down here! Obviously most of them got away. They could still cause us serious trouble."

"The Peacekeeper Lord General believes they have all fled the city," Goorm remarked.

"Generals like victories, and the Peacekeeper Lord General wants a nice, neat victory," said Armindor.

"Well, he won a battle, that is true, but I fear the *war* may not yet be over, and all this celebrating the Lord Director has called for may be premature!" He shivered. "Let us go back aboveground. It is too cold down here for my old bones."

"If there *are* still reen in the city," said Tigg, when they were again on the street in front of Goorm's headquarters, "Reepah and the other grubbers could find out."

"Yes," said Armindor. He rubbed his chin thoughtfully. "You know, he and the other grubbers probably have no idea of what happened last night. They've been keeping pretty much to themselves in the living quarters they were given at the guildhall, and inasmuch as none of them but Reepah understands our language, I doubt that anyone has done much talking to them. I think I shall go and let Reepah know what has happened, and see what he and the others think about it. Perhaps we'll need another sniffing-out check of the city." He glanced down at the two young people. "Want to come with me, or will you be going to the square to join in the festivities?"

Tigg grinned. "Neither. I want to stay here for a while, Armindor. This is where I grew up, you know, and I want to walk around and see some of the places I haven't seen for more than a year."

"I'll stay with Tigg," said Jilla.

"Very well. I'll see you at suppertime," said the magician, and strode off.

"Do you think he's right about there being enough

reen left to still cause trouble?" Jilla asked Tigg when Armindor was out of earshot.

"He's usually right about things," said Tigg. "But I think he'll keep after the Lord Director to do what has to be done to prevent any trouble. If the grubbers find that there are still lots of reen hiding in Ingarron, Armindor will use that as an argument to keep fighting until the creatures are either all killed off or really do flee the city." He grinned. "You can trust Armindor to do what's right, you know that, Jilla."

They wandered about through the shabby oldtown area, which was largely deserted because most of its residents, like those throughout the rest of the city, had gone to the square for the holiday revelries. Tigg pointed out scenes of his life and escapades as a thief and pickpocket. Some sights evoked chuckles and amusement. Others put a grim look on his face. It was with such an expression that he indicated a tiny hovel nestled between two larger dwellings. Its ancient, rotting logs were sagging, and there were holes in the thatched roof.

"That was the only home I ever had until I went with Armindor," said the boy. "Old Paplo's place. I wonder if he's still alive?"

"Who was he?" questioned Jilla. "A relation?"

Tigg vehemently shook his head. "No! Just an old man who got hold of me when I was very little. Not an old man like Armindor, though—a mean, nasty, evil old man! He's the one who taught me how to pick pockets, and when I'd bring enough coins for him to get drunk with, he'd let me sleep on the floor of his house and feed me his leftovers. If I didn't bring enough he'd beat me and push me out to sleep wherever I could and eat whatever I could get—or go hungry." There was bitterness in the boy's voice.

Jilla thought she should change the subject. They had been walking about for the better part of the afternoon, and twilight was now creeping over the city. "We'd better start for home, Tigg. You know how unhappy Armindor gets when someone's late for supper."

"Right," said the boy, and chuckled. "Let's get out of here."

As they turned and started back up the street there was a sudden shout from somewhere nearby, and a woman's voice gave a piercing shriek. Jilla glanced about in concern.

"Don't worry," said Tigg. "They're just celebrating the holiday. Around here they generally celebrate by getting very drunk and fighting. Come on."

Continuing on, they turned a corner. "See?" said Tigg, pointing. "Dead drunk and sleeping it off!" A man lay sprawled in their path, flat on his back, arms and legs flung wide.

But as they neared him, Jilla halted. "Tigg, his eyes are open! He isn't sleeping. He's—he's dead!"

"Somebody probably knifed him, then," muttered the boy. He knelt beside the prone figure and put his fingertips on the man's wrist, feeling for the pulse of a beating heart, as Armindor had taught him. "Yes,

he's dead. But I don't see any wound or blood."
Abruptly he bent forward, bringing his eyes close to
the man's neck. "What's this? Roodemiss! There's a
reen dart in his throat!"

"What?" Jilla reacted with horror to his words. If
the man had been shot by a reen, out here on the
street, then the reen might still be nearby. She realized that darkness was fast closing over the city, and
that was the creatures' natural element. "Tigg, we're
in terrible danger here! We should get away!"

Tigg stood up. "Yes. But—we ought to try to warn
the people around here. Goorm and the others. Armindor was right—I think the reen are coming out
of hiding and looking for revenge!" Suddenly his
head jerked up and his eyes widened as he stared at
something at rooftop level behind the girl. "Roodemiss!"

Jilla spun around, looked up, and gasped. There
was an orange glow in the sky and on some of the
nearest rooftops. She and Tigg became aware of
distant shouting.

"They've started a fire, as they did in Orrello," said
Tigg.

Jilla turned back to look at him and noticed a flicker
of motion off to one side as she did so. She looked
that way—the direction toward which she and Tigg
had been heading when they found the dead man.
No more than half a hundred paces away, a trio of
small shapes, indistinct in the gathering twilight,
moved purposefully toward her and the boy.

"Tigg!" she shrieked, pointing. "Reen!"

He glanced quickly at where she was pointing. "Run!" he yelled. Side by side they sprinted back around the corner they had turned only a short time before.

The street was narrow and winding, so that the end of it could not be seen, but it was clear that it led straight toward the fiery glow that was growing brighter over the rooftops. "We can't go that way," called Tigg. "There's a side street up ahead that will take us out of this part of the city."

But as they turned into the side street they stopped short in their tracks. Three dead people, two men and a woman, lay in contorted postures on the hard-packed dirt surface of the street, and a short distance ahead were five reen. The creatures had their backs to the two children, but at the sounds Tigg and Jilla made as they turned the corner, the reen looked back and saw them. Instantly two of the creatures raised blow-tubes.

"Quick!" yelled Tigg, and he and Jilla darted back around the corner. But they did not dare turn back in the direction they had come from, lest the three reen they had first seen were coming after them. They were forced to continue running toward the fire.

"Wait," called Tigg after they had gone several hundred paces. "Maybe they're not coming after us." The two halted and looked back down the street. "If it looks clear, let's make a run for it back the way we came," said Tigg. "We can't keep going this way or we'll run right into the fire."

Half crouching, they peered back down the shadowed street, praying they wouldn't see any small shapes moving toward them. But after a few moments they saw something else that brought exclamations of horror from both of them. For, back down the street, near the corner they had turned, a bright tongue of orange flame was licking its way up the side of a house. And moments later, a patch of fire appeared on the house directly opposite.

"They've started fires back there, too," said Jilla, her voice quavering. "We don't dare try to get past those burning houses, Tigg; there are sure to be reen near them." She glanced upward, where flaming bits of thatch from the fire behind them were drifting through the air. "We're trapped between two fires, Tigg! If they spread toward us—!"

Tigg stared back at her, his face pale. He knew that in this area, with most of its old buildings formed of ancient, rotting, bone-dry logs, the fires would spread quickly in all directions until all of oldtown was a single gigantic sea of flame. He and Jilla faced a horrible death.

The boy bowed his head. "Help us, Durbis," he pleaded, turning back to the god-spirit he had worshiped before becoming a sage: the god of thieves, who taught his followers to use their wits to get out of dangerous situations. "Help me think of a way to save us. You, too, Roodemiss. Remember, I'm a sage now!"

"Help us, Garmood," Jilla prayed to the god she followed. "Make us able to fly up above the fire."

Tigg lifted his head. "That's it!" he exclaimed, his voice cracking with joy. "We can't fly up above the fire, but we can get down *beneath* it! Thank you, Durbis! Thank you, Roodemiss! Thank you, too, Garmood! Come on, Jilla!"

Seizing the girl by the hand he turned and trotted quickly down the street toward where the main fire was now reaching the rooftops of houses no more than a few hundred paces away. He glanced from side to side, peering intently at the houses they passed on each side of the street.

"What are you going to do?" asked Jilla. She felt sure that Tigg would save them, but she wondered how. What did he mean about getting beneath the fire?

"I'm looking for a house that—ah, that's it, I think. Come on." He led her toward a small, ordinary-appearing dwelling on the north side of the street. He pushed at the door, which swung open with a loud creaking of wooden hinges.

"Hoi, anybody home?" yelled the boy.

There was no answer. "Come on," he said again, urging Jilla inside.

"Should we do this?" she asked, hesitating. "Should we just walk into somebody's house this way?"

"If we don't, we'll burn for sure," he told her, eyeing the brightening glow that was creeping toward them. He followed her in. "Look, the people who live here are probably all at the square, drinking all the berry wine they can hold—or else they're lying dead on the street somewhere nearby. If they're dead they certainly won't care that we're in their house, and if they're at the square their house will probably be burned down by the time they get back."

"But if it's going to burn down why have we come into it?" protested the girl. "I don't understand!"

"We have to find the cellar," he said, peering about in the near darkness of the unlit house. "Here, down this passageway."

There was a door at the end of the passageway. Tigg opened it and made out a flight of crude stone steps leading down into total blackness. "This is it." There was a niche in the wall near the door, where a clay candleholder with a length of candle in it was perched. "Hold this," said Tigg, taking the candleholder and handing it to Jilla. Reaching into an inner pocket of his robe he withdrew a stone and metal sparkmaker and a clay tinderbox. Striking the stone against the bit of metal, he produced a cluster of sparks that set the collection of dry, crumbled leaves and powdery wood in the tinderbox ablaze. Jilla quickly held the candlewick to it.

Tigg waited a moment for the tiny fire in the tinderbox to burn itself out, then replaced the sparkmaker and box in his robe. "All right," he said, taking the candleholder from her. "Pray that I picked the right house!"

Jilla followed him down the steps into a typical old

cellar that had been dug out of the earth and its walls built with rocks and mortar. Tigg moved toward the walls, holding the candle high. The light revealed a wooden door in one wall.

"I was right," said the boy, with satisfaction in his voice. "I thought I remembered that this was a Ratcatcher's house, from when I used to live in this area. Every Ratcatcher's house has a door in its cellar that leads into the tunnels under the city."

He turned to Jilla. "We can stay here. Maybe the fire won't spread to this house, but if it does, we can go through that door into the tunnel. We'll be safe from the fire there, Jilla. We'll live!"

She began to weep with relief. To his surprise, he found himself hugging her and weeping too.

··· 11 ···

The cellar contained no furniture of any kind, so Jilla
and Tigg sat on the bumpy stone floor, near the door
to the tunnels, with their backs up against the wall,
and waited. The candle, which they had placed on
the floor between them, cast a patch of light no more
than a few paces wide, and the rest of the cellar was
completely dark. But after a time, the two youngsters
became aware that a faint reddish light was spreading
through the cellar door, which they had left half-
open, and was creeping down the first few stone steps.
They also noticed a continuous faint rustling sound
and a discernible tang of smoke. And the cellar
seemed to be growing warmer.

Tigg sighed. "I guess the fire has reached the
house. Let me take a quick look and see."

He made his way up the steps and cautiously
peeked around the doorway. A blast of heat struck
him, and the sound that had been a rustling from
down in the basement was now a loud crackling. He
looked down the passageway toward the front of the

house, where he and Jilla had entered. Portions of the plaster that coated the inside of the front wall had fallen away, and the logs that had been behind the plaster could clearly be seen, awash with flames. Smoke filled the passageway, making Tigg's eyes smart and water.

He turned and hurried back down the steps. "Yes, the house is afire," he reported. "It will get bad, soon. We had best go into the tunnel now."

He drew back the wooden bars that bolted the door and tugged it open. A gentle breath of coolness greeted the two as they stepped through the doorway. Although the area beyond the door was not discernibly any blacker than the cellar had been, there was a *feeling* of vast blackness about it, and Tigg and Jilla found they were reluctant to move very far from the doorway, which was visible only as a dim patch of light. But as time passed, this light grew brighter, becoming a pale orange-red shaft that extended into the tunnel. A steady crackling punctuated by frequent sharp pops broke the underground stillness, and an increasing warmth radiated from the doorway, finally becoming so hot that the boy and girl had to slowly give way before it by moving deeper into the tunnel away from the door. The bright glow of light from the door continued to increase, and they were glad for this, for their candle had burned itself out.

There was a sudden roaring crash, and a shower of sparks came swirling through the doorway, followed by a piece of burning log and several glowing fragments of wood that rolled a short distance, then settled on the tunnel floor in a smoldering heap. "The ceiling of the cellar must have collapsed," commented Tigg.

"Those poor people who owned that house," murmured Jilla. "Everything they have will be gone." Then, suddenly, the boy felt her hand close around his arm. "Tigg!" she exclaimed, and he heard stark fear in her voice.

He swung his gaze from the fiery doorway and saw what frightened her. No more than a dozen paces away, in the shadows at the edge of the light coming from the doorway, stood a cluster of some eight reen. They glared at the girl and boy with redly shining eyes.

Tigg felt a cold fear clutch his stomach. We're dead, he thought. We escaped the fire only to die from reen darts down here in the darkness. Well, at least it will be quicker and less painful than the fire would have been. He waited for the creatures to raise their blow-tubes.

But instead, one of them spoke. "Hail, humanss," it said. "How do you like having death and fire come to your own ssity?"

Tigg was not surprised that a reen could speak his language so perfectly, except for a noticeable hissing accent, for he knew that the creatures had long spied on humans and many of them had learned human language. Indeed, both he and Armindor had talked with reen that had conversed with them fluently. But he was surprised that the reen wanted to talk rather than kill the two of them outright. He guessed that it wanted to taunt them first. Well, maybe he could stretch their lives out a little longer by talking with it.

"It is sad to see death and fire come to any community," he said, "whether it be human or reen."

The speaker, which was the reen nearest to Tigg and Jilla, emitted an angry-sounding hiss. "Liar! No human felt any ssadness over what wass done to the reen community! You came with weaponss and fire and ssought to desstroy uss all, utterly!"

"You reen started the war against humans," argued Tigg. "If you had not planned to try to destroy us, we would not have attacked you." Oh, what's the use in trying to argue about right and wrong with them, he thought, and shrugged. "Kill us and get it over with, why don't you?"

The creature pulled its lip back in what looked startlingly like a human sneer. "Maybe we do not wish to kill you," it said. "Do as we ssay, and perhapss we sshall let you live!" It gestured with a clawlike hand. "Kneel."

Tigg stared, confused. Did the creatures simply want to see a couple of humans abase themselves?

"Kneel!" said the reen again, and several of the others raised blow-tubes. "Kneel, or we *shall* kill you!"

"Do it, Jilla," said Tigg in a low voice. "Maybe there's a chance we can live through this. Maybe they just want to see us humble ourselves. As long as we stay alive, Durbis, or Roodemiss—or Garmood—may help me figure out a way to save us." He knelt, and Jilla quickly knelt beside him.

Immediately they were surrounded by the reen. Two of the creatures stood with blow-tubes pointed at each of them.

"Put your hands behind you," directed the reen leader.

Without thinking, the boy and girl obeyed. They felt their hands seized and lengths of what seemed to be thin strands of leather wound around their wrists and tied. Jilla shuddered at the touch of the creatures. Tigg began to feel concern as to what the reen intended.

That his fears were justified was made obvious moments later when pairs of reen on each side of them suddenly shoved them both face forward onto the tunnel floor. Before they could react, more leather strands were whipped around their ankles and tied.

The reen that Tigg had judged to be the leader of the group came and stood before him. Painfully, the boy lifted his head to look at it. Their eyes were level.

"Now," said the reen, "we sshall kill you, humanss. But not quickly, with our dart weaponss. No. We sshall kill you sslowly, with cutting and with fire. Sslowly— with much pain!"

Suddenly its arm flashed at him, and Tigg cried out as pain slashed his cheek. He saw that the reen had a tiny sharp dagger in its hand, and it had sliced him with it. Warm blood was trickling down his chin. Torture, he realized with horror—the reen were going to torture them to death!

··· 12 ···

He heard Jilla gasp in terror. Curse my stupidity, Tigg raged at himself; I should never have let them get us helpless like this! But they won't have an easy time of it—I'll fight, somehow! He struggled to get up onto his feet. But there was a sudden, unexpected interruption.

"*Ssissashoy! Ishkeessa kooshomoo!*"

The strange, hissing words were shouted from somewhere nearby in a reen voice. Involuntarily, Tigg looked toward the sound, as did the reen leader. Another group of reen had appeared. There were seven of them, standing just outside the glow of firelight from the doorway, a short distance away. More torturers, thought Tigg bitterly.

The reen in front of him turned to face them, its body going into a half crouch. "*Ssahmish! Ussissa kooshomoo teess!*" it hissed.

In an instant, to the astonishment of Tigg and Jilla, the two groups of reen had hurled themselves at one another and were fighting—to the death! They all bore wicked little daggers, and that they were skilled in the use of these weapons was obvious. They feinted, parried, made quick underhand thrusts and vicious horizontal slashes. They bobbed, weaved, sought to seize their opponents' knife arms, and used their feet to trip an opponent and knock its legs out from under it.

Tigg managed to struggle back up to his knees and watched the combat while blood dripped from his cheek onto his shoulder. Why are they fighting? he wondered. What does this mean? He could not tell which side was winning, for much of the battle was taking place in darkness, far from the edge of the fireglow, but even if he had been able to see the combatants they all looked alike to him. He could make out three motionless bodies lying on the tunnel floor, and a fourth reen was crawling off into the darkness, its side glistening with blood.

Then, abruptly, the fight was over. There was a shouted word, and a number of the combatants turned and fled. Those remaining—there seemed to be six of them—made no move to follow. One went to one of the dead reen and knelt beside it as if to ascertain that it was indeed dead, then stood up and looked toward Tigg and Jilla. It came toward them and stopped a few paces away. Tigg was fairly sure that it was not the same reen that had talked to him and Jilla and had cut his cheek, for he had noticed that that one had worn a kind of leather belt around its middle, and this one's belt seemed to be of woven cloth.

It spoke. "Humanss, do not fear. We do not intend to harm you."

Well, the other reen had lied, and perhaps this one was lying, too, but Tigg ardently hoped not. He heard Jilla sigh in relief at the creature's words. She, too, had pulled herself to her knees beside him.

"Do not missundersstand," said the reen. "We hate you! We hate you for what you are and for what your kind hass done to uss and our dwelling place. But we will not hurt you, nor kill you. We do not let hatred get in the way of reasson, and we wissh to reasson with you." It pointed a thin, clawed finger at Tigg. "That garment you wear showss that you are one of the group of humanss who sseek the way of wissdom. Iss that right?"

Tigg was faintly surprised that the creatures could tell he was a sage. Obviously, the reen were thoroughly familiar with all the intricacies of human society. "Yes, I am a sage," he answered. "We are seekers of wisdom."

"I thought sso," said the reen. "That iss why we ssaved you from the *shemosh oossimeessu*—those who would destroy all humanss and take their place. We musst sspeak with a human who undersstandss reasson and wissdom. We have a message we wissh you to take to all the humanss."

· 113 ·

"What message?" asked Tigg.

"Firsst, I musst make you undersstand," it said. It cocked its head, eyeing him appraisingly. "Tell me, wissdom sseeker, among humanss iss there ssometimess dissagreement over the way thingss sshould be done?"

"Why, yes," answered the boy. "Often."

"It iss that way, too, among reen. We are ssplit into two groupss that dissagree over the way thingss sshould be done for uss." It gestured toward one of the dead reen. "Thosse we ssaved you from were of the group that believess reen musst desstroy all humanss and take their place in the world. We are of the group known as *asha reen ssessu*—sseekers of the reen way. We do not believe in the war againsst humanss."

Tigg stared at the creature, dumbfounded. It had never occurred to him, or Armindor, or to anyone else who knew anything of the reen, that the creatures might not be united in their desire to wipe out humanity.

"Thosse who want to desstroy humanss and take their place would make the reen become *like* humanss," the reen speaker continued. "They want to use human knowledge and take over human wayss. They want to learn what humanss knew long ago, in that ancient time that you call the Age of Magic. But *we* ssay that sshould not be the reen way. We are not humanss, we are reen! We musst follow our own path, we musst make our own disscoveriess, we musst create our own kind of world. We musst not live off the droppingss of another race of creaturess!" There was anger and contempt in the high-pitched voice.

The creature paused a moment, then went on. "Many reen do not truly belong to either group. They are not quite ssure which way iss right. But for ssev-eral generationss, thosse who would desstroy all hu-manss have been in power in reen communitiess everywhere—they convinced the otherss to let them try their way. And sso, they have long prepared for their war againsst humanss.

"We have argued againsst that war. We believed that if we reen ssuddenly revealed oursselvess and tried to war againsst humanss, we would find them much more dangerouss and determined than thosse who wissh to desstroy them believe them to be. And your attack on our dwelling place sshowed that we were right!

"Now, there iss war among reen! Thosse who sseek to desstroy humanss are dessperately trying to go on with their plan. It iss they who have sset fire to your ssity and who are killing as many of you as they can. But we are trying to sstop them. Not becausse we care about *you*, but becausse we fear that no matter who might win a war between reen and humanss, many reen would be killed and thosse ssurviving would degenerate into groupss at war with each other. All our hopess could be ended!"

It stopped speaking for a moment and moved for-ward, close enough so that Tigg could have reached out and touched it. "Most of thosse who were never

· 115 ·

ssure have now come to our sside," it said. "They can now ssee that we are right. And sso, there iss a chance, a chance that we can gain control and lead all reen in the way we know iss besst for uss. We can end the war against humanss, and we can leave your landss and ssities forever, sso that reen and humanss will never again encounter one another."

"How?" questioned Tigg eagerly.

"There iss a place in thiss part of the world where no humanss live or ever go," it said. "It iss the place you call 'Wild Lands.' We want to make it the home of the reen. We have long argued that reen musst leave human ssities and pay no heed to human wayss. We can live in that land, away from humanss and all human thingss, and sseek our own desstiny!

"Sso, wissdom sseeker, thiss iss the message we want you to take to the other wissdom sseekerss and human leaderss. Tell them all that I have told you. Then tell them there will be no more killing of humanss and no more ssetting of firess, for even now, bands of thosse reen who think as we do are rounding up the groups of thosse who would desstroy all humanss. We will sstop the war against you. If humanss will then sstop their attackss on uss, and let uss leave in peace, we shall go from here, forever. We shall ssend word to the reen of all other communitiess to join uss, and they will, for our way will have proven itsself to be the way of life, and the way of thosse who seek to desstroy all humanss will have been shown to be the way of death. They will have losst their stature, and all other

· 116 ·

reen will turn away from them. *We* will have won, and all other reen will follow uss.

"But, lissten, human—if your fellow-humanss do not accept our offer, if they make another attack againsst the reen, then it iss *we* who will lose sstature, and we from whom all other reen will turn away. For thosse who wish to desstroy all humanss will have been proven right, and they will gain control. Then, the war againsst humanss will go on, until either you or we are wiped away! Make ssure your fellow-humanss undersstand thiss!"

It stopped speaking and stared up at Tigg for several moments. Then it said, "Will you take this message to the otherss of your kind, sseeker of wissdom?"

"Of course," said Tigg. He was overwhelmed at this tremendous opportunity that had fallen his way by sheer chance—unless, of course, it had been arranged by Durbis or Roodemiss. The bargain this reen offered was the best possible solution to the problem between reen and humans. The message he would carry could end the war in a bloodless victory for both sides. Unless—

Unless this was some kind of trick! Unless the reen were just trying to throw humans off guard!

"Come, then," said the reen. "We will lead you to a place where you will be ssafely back in your ssity."

It said something in the reen language to one of its companions, and after a few moments—Tigg could not see how it was done—a tiny flame began to burn in a little clay lamp the other reen held. Tigg took hold of Jilla's hand, and side by side they followed the little light through pace after pace of utter blackness.

"Twice today we've been saved from death," murmured Jilla. "The gods and spirits must be watching over us!" She leaned toward Tigg until her lips were nearly touching his ear and whispered, "Do you think people will believe this message from the reen? It could be a trick."

"I know," he whispered back. "I've been thinking about that." He gave a worried sigh. "We can only tell Armindor and see what he thinks. He'll know what to do."

The journey through darkness seemed to take forever. We must have walked beneath half the city, thought Tigg. Finally, he and Jilla became aware that they were going uphill, as if walking up a ramp.

"Wait a moment," said the voice of the reen. Tigg and Jilla halted. There was a faint grating sound, and they saw a dim patch of grayish light appear in the blackness before them.

"You will have to crawl through," said the reen. "It iss only large enough for uss to walk upright."

Tigg lowered himself to the ground and wriggled through the opening. Scrambling to his feet, he stooped to help Jilla, who was squirming through after him. Glancing up, he saw that the pale gray light was moonlight, slanting through a number of long, narrow windows in what appeared to be a very large, high-ceilinged hall. He realized that they were in the worship house of Garmood. Obviously, the reen had a hidden entrance to the place.

"It iss now the time of ssky-darkness that you call night," said the reen, which had followed them through the opening. "Sstarting with the time of ssky-light that followss thiss dark, you will have five light and dark cycles, or dayss, as you call them, to give our message to your kind and for them to make their decission. We will not be able to control the *shemosh oossimeessu*—thosse who wish to desstroy all humanss—any longer than that. Sso, by the night of the fifth day we musst have an answser. I will be waiting here then, for you to bring it."

The small, indistinct figure vanished into shadows. Once again Tigg and Jilla heard the faint grating noise. Then they were alone, free and safe, in the great empty hall of the house of Garmood.

13

When Tigg and Jilla did not show up at the time when Armindor, who cooked for the three of them, usually had supper ready, the magician was mildly annoyed. Meals were important to him, and he thought others should feel as he did. He waited for a time, and when the two youngsters still did not appear he became slightly concerned. Then he heard people shouting in the street, and went to the door to see what was going on. Many of his neighbors were standing in the street, staring off in the same direction. Armindor turned to see what they were looking at and saw the orange glow in the darkening sky. Obviously, there was a large fire somewhere in the city, which was cause for serious concern.

"Where is it, does anyone know?" he called to the nearest group of neighbors.

"We heard that half the oldtown section is ablaze," a man answered. "The Peacekeepers are there, pulling down nearby houses so the fire won't spread."

Armindor's brow wrinkled into a worried frown.

The oldtown section was, of course, where Tigg and Jilla had been spending the day. Well, he thought, this could explain why they weren't home yet—they were probably watching the fire. Still, it didn't seem like them to stay away so long, even for such an interesting spectacle as burning buildings; they were always very careful not to worry him with unexplained absences, and, knowing how he felt about meals, they always tried to be home in plenty of time.

He went back into his house and sat down to wait, leaving the door half-open. As time went on, his worry grew. He tried to invent many reasons why the boy and girl would be so late, but none of the reasons really explained why they had not returned by now. Finally, the sage had to face the fact that maybe something had happened to them—maybe one of them had been burned, or injured by falling debris from a burning house. He cringed at the thought that they might have been caught in the fire and were, in fact, dead. Once, during the journey to the Wild Lands, he had believed Tigg to be dead, and his grief had been terrible. To think that now he might have lost both youngsters was torture. If that had happened, he did not think he could go on living.

Hours later, at nearly midnight, he was still sitting in the front room of his house, head in hands. He had not bothered to light any lanterns or candles, and the room was only dimly illuminated by a pale shaft of moonlight slanting through the doorway. A kind of murmur filled the city, which was generally silent as a graveyard at this time of night, and Armindor abstractedly realized that it was probably the distant commotion of people fighting to keep the fire from spreading and consuming the entire city. The street in front of his house, also usually silent and empty at night, was filled with the sounds of scurrying feet and anxious voices, as worried people came out of their dwellings to see if the fire was coming closer or was being held in check. And so, Armindor paid little heed as hurrying footsteps approached the house. But suddenly, two dark shapes appeared silhouetted in the doorway. "Armindor?" Tigg's voice softly called. "Are you in here?"

With a cry of joy, the magician flung himself forward, and dropping to his knees, wrapped both youngsters in a single huge hug. "I feared you were dead," he sobbed. "What happened to you?"

"We nearly *were* dead—twice!" said Jilla, hugging him back. "Tigg saved us from the fire, and then we were captured by reen, and—"

"What?" exclaimed the magician. "Captured by reen? How?"

In the darkness they told him everything that had happened. When they had finished, Armindor felt his way over to a table in the corner and fumbled with sparkmaker and tinderbox to light a candle. When it was burning he turned to look at the two youngsters. "This is tremendous news! We must talk about it." He put a hand on his stomach and rubbed gently. "I'm hungry. Are you hungry? I made a good, spicy vege-

· 122 ·

table stew, but I was too worried to eat any of it. I can heat it up for us as soon as I get the cooking fire lit again."

Soon they were all gobbling down bowls of stew and chunks of toasted bread as they discussed the reen message. "Jilla and I fear it could be some sort of trick," said Tigg. "Maybe the reen are just trying to gain time to make a really big attack on us."

"That must be considered," Armindor said. "This offer is going to have to be thought about and talked over very carefully by everybody—sages, the Lord Director, the Peacekeepers, all the others. And we have only five days! I'd best call another big meeting for as quickly as we can get everyone together."

"What about the fire?" asked Jilla. "If the fire is spreading through the city you won't be able to have a meeting. Everyone will either be fighting it or trying to get away!"

"That's true," said Armindor, sounding concerned. "I'd actually forgotten about the fire. Roodemiss curse it, we could lose our whole city along with the chance to end the war and rid ourselves of the reen forever. Everything seems to be against us at the moment."

He slid off his stool and headed to the front door, pushing it open and peering out toward the orange glow in the sky. "It doesn't look any different that I can see," he called. "I can't tell whether it's spreading or not."

He came back into the little eating room. "Well,

there's nothing we can do until morning anyway. We ought to try to get some sleep. Maybe we should drag our mats into the front room. We could leave the door open, and if the fire spreads this way we'd surely be awakened by the commotion of people in the street. We'd have plenty of time to collect what valuables we could and get away."

Following his suggestion, they pulled their sleeping mats into the front of the house and settled themselves. None of them felt they could sleep because of their worry about the fire and their concern over getting the city's leaders together to discuss the reen message. But they were so wearied that they fell right to sleep.

Jilla was awakened by a titanic crash of thunder, and after a moment she became aware of the steady hiss of falling rain. Through the partly open door she could see the gray light of very early morning, and she crept to the doorway and peered out. A torrent of rain was coming down.

"Tigg. Armindor," she called. "Look at all this rain. Surely it will help put out the fire."

Tigg, awake in an instant, joined her at the door, poking his head far enough out so that he could look in the direction of the fire. "There's a huge cloud of smoke hanging over that part of the city, but I don't see any sign of fire," he reported.

"Thanks be to Roodemiss," rumbled Armindor, rising stiffly to his feet and rubbing his eyes. "Maybe they got it under control, and everyone will be able to think about other things! Well, heavy rain or not, I've got to get to the guildhall and set things in motion for another meeting. Even if we can get everyone together by tomorrow, there'll be only four days left, and I'm afraid it's going to take a lot of talking to decide whether to accept the reen offer or not."

··· 14 ···

Once again the great Hall of Discussions of the Sages'
Guildhall of Ingarron was packed with people. Armindor's message that an offer to end the war had
been made by the reen was received with differing
emotions by the various leaders of the city, but all
had realized the importance of meeting to talk about
the offer. It was common knowledge that the attack
on the reen community had not wiped out most of
the creatures and driven away the rest, as had first
been thought, for nearly a fifth of Ingarron now lay
burnt and gutted by the fires known to have been set
by the reen, and more than a hundred people had
been killed by the creatures or had perished in the
fire. There was no doubt that a full-scale war was
raging and Ingarron was a battleground.

When everyone was finally present and seated, Armindor spoke to them, reporting how Tigg and Jilla
had been captured by one group of reen and rescued
by another whose leader had made the offer that all
reen would leave the lands of humans and settle in

the Wild Lands if the humans would promise not to hinder or attack them. "This seems like an incredibly perfect answer to our problem with the reen," said Armindor, "but obviously we must thoroughly talk it over and think it through. It is now noon; we have three and a half days before Novice Sage Tigg must meet with the reen leader and deliver our answer." He bowed in the direction of Lord Director Mogariom. "Your Greatness, I leave the leadership of this meeting in your hands."

Mogariom nodded, and banged sharply on the floor with the end of his long, carved wooden staff of office to indicate that the meeting had officially begun. "Who would speak?" he asked, glancing about.

One of the Councilors seated near him, an elderly, sour-faced man, raised a hand, and the Lord Director gestured to him. "Speak, Councilor Doyalim."

"I say that these reen creatures are obviously lying about wanting to go to the Wild Lands," said the man, rising to his feet. "Everyone knows what a terrible place the Wild Lands is—full of monsters, deadwalkers, and poisonous fogs and deadly plants! It would be too dangerous for the reen to try to live there, and they don't really intend to! It's a trick!" He sat down.

Armindor raised a hand, and the Lord Director nodded to him. "Speak, High Master Armindor."

"I can assure you all," said Armindor, first looking earnestly at Councilor Doyalim and then letting his gaze swing about the room, "that those tales you've heard of the Wild Lands simply are not true. I have been there, and I know. There are dangerous wild animals living there, yes, but as for monsters and deadwalkers and all the rest, that's just nonsense. Creatures as clever and well-armed as the reen could easily live there."

The Peacekeeper Lord General raised his hand, and the Lord Director indicated he could speak. The dark-skinned Peacekeeper rose to his feet.

"It may well be true that the reen could live in the Wild Lands," he acknowledged. "But we must still consider carefully whether this reen offer could be a trick. Suppose we agree to it, and the reen go marching away from Ingarron. As time passed, we would certainly let our guard down—reduce the number of Peacekeepers, put our armor and special weapons away in the armory, and go back to the way things were before we knew about the reen and felt we were perfectly safe. But what if the reen did *not* really march away to the Wild Lands, but were simply hiding nearby somewhere and biding their time—and when our guard was completely down, what if they suddenly returned and attacked? We would be caught unprepared and wiped out like the people of Orrello!"

"Do you counsel that we refuse the reen offer, then?" asked the Lord Director.

The Peacekeeper smiled, showing his teeth. "Oh, no indeed, Your Greatness. I suggest that we accept. And then, when the creatures are leaving Ingarron, unsuspecting and unprotected, we fall upon them with spears, clubs, and fire bottles, and wipe them out! In other words I suggest that we do to them what they plan to do to us!"

Among the blue-robed sages a hand shot up. The Lord Director pointed toward it. "Speak, Your Wisdom."

The sage stood up. He was a slim, youngish man with a bushy black beard who was dark skinned like the Peacekeeper. "But we do *not* know for sure that is what they plan to do to us, Lord General," he protested. "That is only your *guess*. If the reen offer is an honest one, and we do what you suggest, we will be guilty of dreadful betrayal! We would be completely in the wrong, and would shatter forever any chance of peace!"

"Bah!" The Lord General gave a contemptuous wave of his hand. "What you call 'betrayal' is a legitimate act of warfare that has been done by armies countless times in history. And it would actually *bring* peace. We would crush the reen so badly they probably *would* flee to the Wild Lands, and we'd never be bothered with them again."

Armindor sighed audibly and raised his hand. The Lord Director indicated him, and he rose.

"I must point out, Lord General, that we had one attempt at 'crushing' the reen and were unable to do so. We had all the tunnels blocked off and still most of the creatures managed to escape. What makes you think you could do better out in the open, where the reen would have an even better chance of fleeing to safety?"

The Peacekeeper scowled. "We would surround them. It could be done."

"Perhaps," said Armindor, but his voice implied strong doubt. "However, I think you would agree that even a few of them might escape. And if they did, would they not carry word of our betrayal to the reen of other communities? That would hardly bring about peace! More likely we would soon find ourselves facing an army of reen from other communities, come to punish us for our betrayal of their kin."

The Peacekeeper scowled again but made no reply. Armindor sat down.

One of the russet-robed merchants raised a hand. "Isn't there some way we can figure out for sure whether the reen offer is truly sincere? We merchants examine every move we make in terms of whether it would be most likely to bring a profit or loss. Would it be more to the creatures' profit to go to the Wild Lands or to try to trick us and attack us as the Lord General thinks they might do?"

The Lord General's hand shot up. "Trickery would be more to their profit," he assured the merchant. "If they could catch us unawares and wipe us out as they did the people of Orrello, they would no longer be in any danger from us."

The gray-sleeved arm of a priestess of The Mother of All went up. "It would profit them more to go to the Wild Lands," she stated, frowning at the Peacekeeper. "They would lose no lives that way, but in an attack on us, even if they caught us by surprise, some of them would surely be killed."

"That would not matter to them, if they look upon warfare in the same way we do," the Lord General retorted. "Every military leader accepts the fact that soldiers will be lost in battle—perhaps many of them. But it is the *result* that counts, and if the reen could catch us unawares and wipe us out, that result would be well worth the loss of many of them!"

Lord Director Mogariom gnawed at his lip and peered about the room. "Are the two young ones who brought the reen message here in the chamber?" he asked. Tigg and Jilla, who were seated among the sages, stood up. As a sage, Tigg of course was automatically included in the meeting, and Armindor had felt justified in letting Jilla be present because she had been directly involved with the message from the reen. The Lord Director leaned forward toward them. "Tell us exactly what happened from the time the reen captured you to the time they set you free— everything they did and everything they said. Perhaps we can gain a hint as to whether there's truth or treachery in this offer of theirs."

Tigg told the whole story, glancing at Jilla from time to time to see if she agreed with his recollection of things. When he finished he hesitated for a moment, then, speaking to the Lord Director, said, "I think that most of what the second reen told us was probably true, Your Greatness. He said there were rival groups among the reen, and we certainly saw his group and the other one fighting and killing each other. And he certainly sounded as if he meant it when he said his group wanted to get away from humans and not ever use any of our things. If that was true, maybe it's all true."

"It could have all been plotted in advance," suggested the little, sharp-faced Councilman next to Mogariom. "You said you were in almost complete darkness down there; perhaps the creatures weren't really fighting at all, and when the second group led you away, all the 'dead' reen simply got up and dusted themselves off. Perhaps the whole thing was staged in advance, like a puppet show, to make you believe everything the reen told you was true!"

"That hardly seems possible," said the brown-robed high priest of Garmood. "How could they have possibly known that these two children were going to seek refuge in that cellar and go into the tunnel? It was obviously all pure chance. It seems clear to me that the reen offer is an honest one. I counsel that we accept it." There were murmurs of agreement among the crowd.

The Lord General sprang to his feet without raising his hand. His eyes were blazing. "How can we possibly agree to let these rat-things simply go off free and unpunished? Most of oldtown is destroyed by their fires and scores of people are dead from their poisoned darts. The blood of those dead Ingarronians cries out for vengeance! We must not give up a war that I tell you we can *win!* The creatures were helpless against us when we attacked their underground city; we must attack again, rout them out of their hiding places in the tunnels, and wipe them out once and for all!" There were sounds of agreement for his words, too, from others in the crowd.

Angrily, the Lord Director banged his carved staff on the floor. "Silence! Let no one else speak out of turn! Nothing will be gained if we all begin arguing at once!" The murmurs subsided and he leaned back in his chair. "It seems to me that we have reasonably well established that the reen offer is an honest one, but that some of you feel we should continue to make war on the creatures nevertheless. This, then, is what we must decide on."

Several hands went up, and one of them was Armindor's. It was at him that the Lord Director pointed. "Speak, High Master Armindor."

Armindor climbed to his feet. For a moment or two he said nothing, letting his gaze roam over the faces that were turned toward him from all parts of the room. Then, he began.

"In order to decide this matter properly," he said, "I think we must consider what took place in the Age of Magic. Even those of you who are not sages and who have never studied the past know something of that time, some three thousand years ago. People then had knowledge and magic and power that made their world a place of wonder that we can scarcely imagine. You have all heard the old, old tales of how they could fly, how they could talk to one another across enormous distances, how they could travel thousands and thousands of paces in less than half a day, and of other wonders.

"But wonders such as those were not the most important things of the Age of Magic. What were more important were the things that made peoples' lives better, safer, happier, more pleasant than the lives of most of us today can be. They did not have *half* their babies die in the first few years of life, as we do, bringing sorrow to parents. They did not have to fear famine and food shortages, as we often do—if the old stories are true, they actually had more food than they could even eat! They did not suffer from the scores of different killing and crippling diseases we all fear. They lived far longer than we do. They were healthier and happier. They had so much!

"But you all know of the Fire from the Sky, which brought their world to an end. We are not quite sure what the Fire from the Sky was, but most sages think it was probably a *weapon*. They think that the Age of Magic was brought to an end by warfare. Despite their magic and knowledge, those ancient people— our ancestors—destroyed themselves with warfare, and most everything they had was lost.

"In the thousands of years since then, sages have labored to try to regain what knowledge we could from the Age of Magic. We've learned a bit here and a few things there, but it hasn't amounted to the tiniest portion of what people had then. The main problem has always been that we just could not understand most of the old writings that had been preserved. Not only is our language very different from the language our ancestors spoke three thousand years ago, but they also used many words for things that we simply have no knowledge of now. Who knows what is meant by such words as 'atoms, 'electricity,' 'trigonometry,' 'radiation'? They are mysteries we thought we could never hope to solve."

Armindor's face had been sober as he spoke, but suddenly he broke into a smile. "But now I can tell you that a way to learn the ancient language has been found! When Novice Sage Tigg and I came back from the Wild Lands, where we went to search for ancient spells, we brought with us an old, old sealed box from the Age of Magic. In Inbal, with the help of the sages there, the box was opened. It turned out to be the most wonderful, marvelous spell of magic that was ever found! *A voice speaks from it,* the voice of a magician of the Age of Magic, saying words in the ancient language. And on a part of the box, pictures appear as each word is spoken, showing what the word means! The sages of Inbal are even now working night and day to copy the words and their meanings in our own tongue, and so soon we shall have a way to translate all the old writings. We can finally learn how to do many of the things that can make our lives better, that can pull us up out of the dirt and the stink and the sickness and hunger, to a *new* Age of Magic!"

He paused, and his expression grew sober again. "One of the main reasons why I urged you to make war on the reen was because I feared that unless we conquered them before they conquered us, this great dream of rebuilding our world could never come true. I feared that the reen might wipe us out, and the secrets of our ancestors would pass into *their* hands. Now, suddenly, I see a chance to be sure the dream can come true! If there can be peace, if we can become free of the danger of attack by the reen, we will surely be able to begin doing the things we can learn to do because of the box from the Age of Magic. But if the war with the reen goes on, all our hopes may be ended. It was warfare that destroyed the Age of Magic, but we must not let warfare destroy our chance to regain what was lost then." He held out a hand, as if begging. "And so, I plead with you all— let us agree to the reen offer! Let them go in peace, and let us begin the work of rebuilding our world!"

Armindor sat down. There was a long silence. Finally Master Sage Dalinda raised his hand.

"Speak," said Lord Director Mogariom.

"I ask that you call for a show of hands of those who would agree to accept the reen offer," said Dalinda.

Mogariom nodded. "Let all those who would agree to let the reen depart in peace now raise their hands," he called.

Tigg held his breath, but there was no need to worry. All around the chamber hands were going up, and it was clear that the overwhelming choice was for accepting the offer the reen had made. Only a few people did not raise their hands, among them the Lord General of the Peacekeepers, who was staring at the floor as if deep in thought. Abruptly, he looked up, straight at Armindor, and thrust up his hand.

"So shall it be," intoned Lord Director Mogariom, and struck the heel of his staff on the floor with a thump. "On the appointed day, let Novice Sage Tigg carry word to the reen that we accept their request and that they may depart from the city of Ingarron and the lands of humans, unhindered."

Tigg found himself wriggling with delight. The war was over, and it actually looked as if both humans and reen had won! Perhaps someday we can even be friends with them, thought the boy, as we are with the grubbers. And as for the grubbers, things would be safer and better for them, too, once the reen left this part of the world. There were grubbers in the Wild Lands, but that was a vast region, and there was room for both them and the reen. It seemed as if events were turning out well for everyone!

He looked at Armindor. He knew, with a deep touch of sadness, that someday the old man would be gone, but there were people in Inbal and Ingarron who would never forget all the things he had done for them, and for people everywhere. And *I* shall certainly never forget him, thought Tigg. I vow with all my heart that I'll be the kind of sage he wants me to be—the kind *he* is. I vow that I'll work my head off to see that his dream of making a better world comes true!

Armindor looked at him and grinned. Tigg grinned back. He felt Jilla's hand slip into his, and turned to look into her pretty, smiling face. It seemed to him that the future was as bright as the dawn of a sunny summer day.